A SWARM OF DUST

I0653624

EVALD FLISAR

A SWARM
OF DUST

Translated from the Slovene by David Limon

istrosbooks

First published in 2018 by
Istros Books
London, United Kingdom www.istrosbooks.com

First published in Slovenia by Sodobnost International as *Greh* (*Sin*), 2017

David Limon has received a translation grant from the Slovenian Book Agency.

Cover design and typesetting: Davor Pukljak, www.frontispis.hr

ISBN: 978-1-908236-38-8

Published with the financial assistance of Trubar Foundation, Ljubljana, Slovenia.

PART ONE

There was a full moon. Through the sparse branches of the pine trees it cast its light among the buildings. The meadows beside the stream were a silvery grey. The whole landscape had been transformed into sharp-edged patches of light and dark. Janek spent a long time crouching at the lower edge of the woods, despite the unpleasant night chill and the constant, unfathomable feeling that his surroundings were strange in some special way.

He stared at the sky. Hints of thoughts flashed through his brain, but he was unable to connect them. This strange state had overcome him the moment that the landscape began to seem unusual and his eyes drank in the visible objects. His feelings dragged him along. He saw the silvery meadow in the valley and the dark track of alder by the stream. He knew that was what he was seeing, but that was all he knew, his mind was somehow distant. Normally when he saw meadows and a stream he thought about something, objects aroused different associations that were either whole or fragmented and scattered, but always thoughts and impressions found their way through. He would skip from grass to stream, to trees, to children chasing each other among the trees, to felling trees, to scooping water from the stream, and all these thoughts and impressions triggered associations that swarmed within him.

Now the mental state of young Hudorovec was completely different. It happened just after he was struck by the unusual colour of the meadows. This halted the flow of associations that would at any moment have engulfed him and he focused entirely on the meadows and their appearance. He began to soak up this appearance, he began to soak up the colour and he felt the silvery colour was coming closer to him. He could sharply smell the night chill. It was the dampness coming from the valley, the damp earth, the damp grass, the dampness of the lazily flowing water, damp bark, leaves damp with dew, the dampness of the air.

And he heard a fox yelping in the woods, he heard the gentle wind moving the leaves in the treetops, slowly flowing through them and making them tremble. He felt how the wind swept across the damp grass, shaking it slightly, how it licked the clods of earth in the fields, how it slightly ruffled the surface of the stream, how it caused the tiny scales on the tree bark to tremble a little, how it flowed through the air. He felt the ruffled coat of the fox and its hoarse call, he felt the mossy ground beneath its paws, he felt the stickiness of the fat, slippery footbridge across the stream and the solidness of the ground beneath him.

He felt the expanse of the world, its hollowness, its extensiveness, he felt the distance of the sky above him and the closeness of the earth and its objects, he felt the form, the hardness and softness of substances and things, he sensed the tone of the sounds rushing to his ears. And he smelt all of this: he smelt the sap of the trees, the smell of the earth, the spruce needles, the brushwood, he smelt the smoke, he felt how the water in the stream smelled of mud and acorns, he smelt the warm plumage of birds, he smelt the wood close to him, his clothes, his skin, he smelt the stench from the woods, he smelt sweat.

Behind him, in the settlement, a radio began to play. He knew that Pišta Baranja had a radio, but he did not know this as a thought, but rather felt it in a particular way, like the self-evident fact that water is wet and that your hand will also be wet if you plunge it in.

That the radio he could hear belonged to Pišta Baranja was alive in him like something for which there was no other explanation; something self-evident that touched the edge of awareness like a shadow, but a distinct shadow. And so he only heard the music coming from the radio; it did not draw him into any associations in connection with the music, the radio, the settlement. For him, the sounds were movements of matter and he grasped them in the same way he grasped the colour of the meadows, the stench of dirt, the rustling of the wind.

Getting up and moving towards the settlement was a highly complex process of sensory perceptions and movements of matter. Perhaps the cold played the main role, but he could not say so with any certainty. Among the feelings bursting and splashing within him, the feeling of coldness was ever more frequent; after first appearing of its own accord, it then began to attach itself to others, it pierced him with a feeling of dampness – with a feeling of the wind, with a feeling of the stickiness of a tree trunk, with a feeling of the yellow light – and when a dog barked above him in the settlement it also awoke in him a feeling of coldness. The earth beneath him soon lost its hardness and roughness, and changed into a feeling of coldness. And when his stomach grumbled he felt his body, he felt its substance, he felt his posture, his stillness, he felt the possibility that he might move, he felt the pulse within him. In the veins on his neck his blood pulsed, and he felt how it flowed and at the same time felt how coldness flowed through him. He got up and went towards the buildings.

Of course, it wasn't that simple, for when someone who has been sitting motionless suddenly moves it is likely that some idea came upon him and triggered the desire for movement. And when someone feels cold, it is natural to be aware of this and to think: it's cold, better get moving. This didn't happen in the case of Janek Hudorovec, since he didn't move with any intention. Wave a stick at a dog and he will jump, offer a bunch of hay to a cow and it will move towards you, frighten a wolf and you should flee, for it will leap at your throat! Perhaps Janek Hudorovec instinctively retreated from the coldness, just as an animal drags itself towards a fire or its den. He acted under some kind of delusion, but in spite of this everything remained clear: objects and his perception of them. In the same way that he had felt cold, he now felt warmth, flowing beneath the bed cover.

He was not aware of time, but when his mother entered the house he saw that the moon was still shining through the small window, illuminating part of the wall and floor, but not his bed, which was in darkness. His mother put down the basket in which she had just brought the potatoes, flour and bread that she brought every evening. Then she went to her bed, which was lit by the moon, knelt down, turned back the cover and with her right hand straightened the pillow. Then she took the basin that was leaning against the wall by the door and put it on the wooden bench. There was a slight metallic noise as she did so. Then the sound of water being poured from a jug. The moon shone on her and the corner where she was standing. She reached for her belt, unfastened buttons and began to undress. She hung her clothes on a nail hammered into the wooden wall; then she began to splash herself with water and wash her naked body. Janek could see her clearly, but now his mother's naked body filled him with no more feeling than had the silvery meadow or the outline of the trees. He perceived her body as substance.

The scent of soap reached him, he heard rubbing as his mother washed her feet. She lifted one and stood on the other. He saw her large breasts shaking, he saw the roundness of her belly shining, and when she rubbed her back with a towel she leaned slightly backwards. He saw the blackish shadow beneath her belly. None of this seemed unusual to him, he was cut off from experience. And so he could not be surprised that his mother had stripped off in front of him. The thought could not take hold that maybe she did not see him and was convinced that he was not there.

Then she put the towel down on the bench, left the water in the basin, rummaged among the things on the edge of the bench, found some scissors, went over to her bed, sat down, bent over and began to cut her toenails. With each one he heard a slight click.

The moon shone on her back. Janek could see her vertebrae, dividing her back into two halves. When she had finished her toenails, she lay back, raised her hands in front of her face and began on her fingernails. Once again, they could be heard hitting the wall and the floor.

Then she stopped for a moment, placed her hands beside her and looked at the ceiling, as if in thought. Janek could hear her breathing. He could see the slight rise and fall of her breasts. It seemed as if she was trembling a little. Probably the cold was getting to her. But she still lay there without getting under the cover.

What happened within him that he suddenly got up and moved towards her? Our interior world is such an anthill of perceptions, feelings, thoughts, emotions and impulses that at certain moments, even with the sharpest eyes, it is not possible to penetrate it. Allowing for the possibility that we might be wrong, we might say that within young Hudorovec in those moments when he was cut off from experiencing, there expired all the strange anxiety that women and sexuality evoked within him. When the sensory and perceptual world prevailed, weakening his mental capacities, his instincts became stronger and his reactions began to resemble the reactions of animals, guided by the impulses of the real world. At such moments his sexual drive must have been stronger. We all know how dogs behave; we've all seen them pairing on the road in full sight. First the sniffing, then the running, the agitation, a kind of wooing, in between some snapping and sharp teeth, hackles rising, and finally the submission of the female and the action of the male. All this happens without the presence of the mental world, it happens beneath the wings of the sensual, within the framework of instinct.

When Janek shuffled over to his mother's bed, he certainly wasn't struggling with fear, with indecisiveness. He was not clear what he was doing, since he had never done anything like this before. He was being drawn to his mother's naked body on the bed, just as the animal male is drawn towards the female when he sees or smells her. His mother started in fright and exclaimed: 'Janek!'

In young Hudorovec's mind associations were triggered: his mother's shriek was like the hoarse bark of the fox he had heard in the woods. But that was just a momentary flash that quickly vanished. He was not aware of his mother's fright, he did not perceive it. He touched her body, which trembled, he felt the smoothness of her skin, he felt the warmth, her smell. He ran his hand over her belly, across the dark shadow beneath it, to the thigh, the knee, then back, to the breast, the neck. All his sensations condensed into one: the hot pulse of blood, the tension of the body yearning to explode, the absence of any thought, impetus, a feeling of flying, a feeling of falling and rising.

In each person, in the most intense sexual spasm, there is a small spark that draws attention to the nature of the act in which he and some other person is present. In young Hudorovec this was absent. He was completely in the domain of sensation. After a brief trembling brought on by her son's strange behaviour, his mother experienced a kind of spasm. The next cry that came from her throat was one of unknown joy. A strange heat washed over her, she held Janek's body, which was no bigger than hers and very thin, and then she began to tear his shirt off, crying out and whispering strange words, as if hallucinating.

'Don't be scared, Janek… don't be afraid… we all do this and you must, too… my heart would pain me if you didn't… don't be afraid… I'm your mother… I'll show you how… you'll see, you'll see…' Suppressed gasps mingled with her words, as she stripped him completely with hungry hands. 'You see, in here.' She turned him towards her, locking him with her legs, grabbing his hair and wildly kissing his eyes. She raked her fingers across him, all the while gasping, panting and whispering. At the beginning Janek only breathed deeply, but then strange sounds emerged from his throat, a strangled noise. He took hold of his mother's hair and roughly pulled her towards him.

'Ow, that hurts, Janek…' she sighed. 'But let it hurt, let it hurt… it's nice if it hurts.' Then he bit into the skin on her shoulder and she cried out in pain, he began to slap her, to beat her all over so that she was gasping. 'Hit me, Janek… hit me… more… you're a good boy, Janek… you must beat me, you must punish me, you must always beat me… till my dying breath I'd do anything for you… Janek… my son…' Towards the end she wheezed, his spasm ended, he unclenched his fists, he lay on her body, then he rolled aside. He saw that she was bloody from his bites and mottled from the blows. He looked at his own body, his member, which seemed red in the moonlight. An association immediately flashed into his brain, as he remembered the red tongue of a panting dog by the stream.

Then something snapped inside him. Thoughts rushed upon him. Through the bustle there trickled all that he had experienced, all that had stifled him. With all these dark feelings inside him, he turned to his mother's bitten body, their nakedness. An image of his actions began to appear: he remembered he had beaten his mother… he felt dizzy, objects slipped away from him… his ears were filled with silence, he passed out.

When he came to, he was lying beneath the cover on his own bed. His mother was leaning over him and dabbing his face with a wet cloth. She was dressed. Previous feelings overwhelmed him again. They choked him, then they flowed away, the dark mass shattered, and he began to sob, convulsively and silently. 'Janek!' she said, 'you mustn't cry. You must go to sleep. Then it'll be all right. Everything'll be all right!' The sobbing became a long, inconsolable cry. His mother stroked his cheeks for a while and then she threw herself on the bed beside him and began to sob too. When they had no tears left, their bodies shook with silent convulsions. The spasms gradually became sparser.

A coldness began to grow between them.

Summer came, dry and windy. There was no rain; it seemed as if the countryside would burn up in the drought. Old Baranja deteriorated, his skin turned yellow and limp, he was shrivelling into a skeleton. He spoke to no one, he hid in his house and no one saw him the whole week. Sometimes he could be heard cursing, throwing things at the wall and choking as he coughed. It seemed as if he could pass away at any minute, but Baranja fought back.

In the evening, when the sun was no longer so fierce, he appeared once again in front of his house and lifelessly lingered on the threshold. He was no longer coughing so badly. Emma had to bring him schnapps. Whenever he sat outside, the bottle was beside him.

In early July three gypsies came, two Horvats and a Šarkezi. They were tired and morose looking, they threw their wooden suitcases down in the corner and grimly said they had been let go. More soon followed. They began to sit around in front of their houses; the settlement began to change into a mortuary. School kids started wandering around the villages all day as the school year had ended. The sun on the dried-out front yards was dazzling. Even in the shade of the trees it was insufferably hot. No one spoke, the gypsies moved slowly and lazily, sleeping most of the time, and even the dogs no longer barked, but lay around, tongues lolling. People were overcome by a dull lethargy. They spoke with great difficulty and hoarsely, opening their mouths only when it was unavoidable, and then only half way.

During the day Janek did not hang around the settlement. He suddenly had the feeling that a stench of dirt, sweat and inertia was coming from the houses. The smell was nothing new, he had smelt it before, but now it began to disturb him, to make him feel nauseous. Beneath the hot sun the smell was particularly intolerable, it hung in the air among the trees and made it difficult to breathe. Maybe the smell was also an excuse, since he did not want to linger. Maybe he dared not admit to himself that he was being driven from the settlement by something else, a kind of fear that he would speak to someone, that he would make eye contact with someone, for he was filled with what felt like guilt and beneath the hot sun among the buildings that feeling was very strong, insupportable.

If he was not lying in the grass down by the stream, he was wandering through the woods, which in that hot summer were unusually quiet. Sometimes he was lured far away, across the valley and into the hills on the eastern side, even straying onto the lowland. Now and then he sat on some rotting tree stump to rest and then he was driven on again aimlessly, he stopped by streams and watched them, he looked at the trees and touched their crusty trunks; sometimes he scared a hare out of the bushes, which went crashing into the woods, another time a whole column of deer passed by. He cooled down and quenched his thirst at forest springs. Whenever he came to the edge of the trees, he stopped and looked at the landscape before him, then turned and went back. He did not walk across fields, orchards or meadows, he kept to the woods where he was seen by no one, where he felt alone with the damp silence and the sappy smell of wood.

During this wandering, the feeling of anxiety was not so intense, it became a deadness, a laziness of the arteries, a numbness of body and mind. Thoughts flowed idly through him, like the forest streams running among the dry grass. This numbness lasted quite some time, but now and then it was interrupted by sudden outbursts of sharp and unfamiliar feelings. Sometimes he was overwhelmed by an undermining fear and he did not know its source, nor did he even try to work it out, but rather succumbed to it with a trembling sense of enjoyment. Other times he was overcome by a shrill sense of joy. He would roll on the moss, run his hands over tree bark, hug their trunks, leap around and yell, and then chase the echo from the woods. But in a moment it all vanished, as in a whirlpool, and then everything flowed back to its former lethargy, to the dead decanting of thoughts, to the endless wandering through the woods.

He always returned late at night. And every night he and his mother pleased each other. It usually lasted until morning, when she went into the village to work and he disappeared on his familiar paths. They barely spoke; sometimes they whispered as if afraid they might wake someone, but even that was rare. They were scared they might say something loud enough to break something, destroy it. The whole time they had the feeling that what they were doing was mysterious and that it could bear no voices, apart from the cries and gasps emitted during lovemaking.

At night his spiritual lethargy was transformed into sharp sensations that had hitherto been alien to him. He still beat his mother, tormenting her more every night. When he heard her gasp with pain he felt a particular passion. It was not unlike that time when he and Pišta Baranja had killed the puppies that no one wanted. They were little fluffy balls, still blind, crawling over each other and squealing and shaking their snouts, and when he touched them he felt how warm the little creatures were and how their blood was pulsing just below their skin. When Pišta Baranja grabbed the first one by its leg and bashed it against a tree, he broke out in sweat and felt fixed to the ground. This was despair or something like it, a kind of fear at incomprehensible action, but the more the fear grew, the more another feeling grew alongside it that suppressed the fear. And when that feeling prevailed, he leapt on the little creatures, trembling, saliva dripping from his mouth, his eyes glassy, and he bashed one puppy against the tree for so long that he shattered its blind head and reduced its body to pulp. Then he put his hand into the bloody mass of flesh and groped it.

Making love with his mother filled him with a similar feeling; he tortured her until she bled and the more she panted with desire, the stronger grew the wish to make her suffer as much as possible. So she no longer felt enjoyment, but a kind of torment. The wildness of their relationship grew from night to night. When by chance they saw each other during the day he looked at her glassy-eyed, feeling a tremulous fear of her, but at the same time an intense hatred. The whole time he was gripped with a desire to torture her. She stared at him with docile humility. The whole time she reminded him of those crawling puppies, tumbling over each other. When on occasion he was weary of rushing through the woods and lay down on the moss and closed his eyes, he saw her convulsive movements, her distorted face in the moonlight, he heard her cries, and all this swirled together inside him, creating strange images, fading away and then returning. And when he walked among the trees all that floated before his eyes were images of their coupling, every object reminded him of some shade of night and he was flooded with the desire to hit, to beat, to torment.

One evening, he didn't know how, he returned home before dark. The sun was going down behind the hill, but it was still quite light. In front of Baranja's house he saw Emma walking to and fro. He realised she was hanging clothes on a line between two pine trees. On the bench in front of the house was a wooden tub and she had just finished doing the washing. He saw her look at him as soon as he emerged from the trees and the whole time she watched him as he continued towards home. He was about to go inside when he heard her calling him. He stopped, but then moved quickly forward. 'Janek!' she called again, louder this time. 'Come here, something's happened to your mother.' He was struck as if by lightning. He looked up, towards her, his legs took him in her direction, but something held him back. Emma wiped her hands on her apron and then kept beckoning with her finger. Her face bore a mysterious expression.

'Come,' she said and disappeared round the corner, then up into the woods. He followed her. His every vein was taut, and confused feelings flowed through him. When they got to the edge of the woods at the top of the slope she whispered to him to go quietly, and without meaning to he began to put his feet down without making a sound. Emma stopped behind some dense acacias and gestured to him again, then she pointed through the bushes. He came closer.

Behind the thorns and brambles, around a large white hornbeam was a bed of moss. His mother was kneeling there, smoothing her creased skirt. Then she buttoned up her blouse. Beside her stood a tall, thin farmer, fastening his trousers. It was Geder. His mother picked up the basket that was leaning against the hornbeam and looked at Geder, but said nothing. They both turned and left, Geder to the left, towards the nearby road, his mother towards the gypsy settlement. Long after the rustle of her steps faded, Janek remained staring at the tree and the moss beneath it. The only feeling that gripped him at that moment was contempt for Geder, for he was certain that the man had not beaten his mother and so she would not be satisfied. Her words came back to him: you must beat me… then it is better…

Geder did it just like that, as if mother meant nothing to him? Just like that? The past, from which he'd been cut off for so long, assailed him and he slumped to the ground, seething with memories. Images appeared and vanished. He saw how once, in those other places, in school, he had stolen a large piece of bread from some farmer's girl, how he had flown home with this bread, where his mother was ill and there was nothing to eat, and his father and sister were ignoring her; he saw how he fell to his knees beside her bed and shoved the dried up bread into her hand and said: bread, mother, bread... eat it.. And he remembered how he felt when he sat in the corner and watched his mother chewing the bread and looking at him with bright eyes. It was like a strange trembling, a yelling within him. And before him danced the priest, the one here... do you love your mother, he asked... Love, love... He broke into a sweat, he realised he felt something different towards his mother than he had before and he was overcome with torment at the memories. It all seethed inside him. The sense of confusion was so strong that he could not see clearly. He got up again and the contempt for Geder reappeared, for he should have beaten her, otherwise she was not happy. And mother must be happy. He felt tears running down his cheeks. Mother... he sobbed inside. He would always beat her, he would always yield to her, he would always do what she wanted.

Through his tears he saw Emma crouching beside him, looking at him in fright. But there was also a kind of mockery in her eyes. 'Janek,' she said, 'didn't you know? They've been doing it for ages. Will you tell your father?' Amazement grew within him. Emma talked on; he didn't quite know what she was saying, but some of her words struck him sharply. 'If they can, so can we... I'd like to... do you want to, Janek, my husband's away... Janek... do you want to...?'

'You don't understand!' he yelled, startling her. He saw her wide open eyes, he saw her timidly withdraw. He was filled with confusion, it stirred within him, disintegrated. He was thrown upwards, and then down into the woods, where it was already getting dark...

That night he was wild like never before. He bit his mother's breasts and shoulder, drawing blood. Then at the end he whispered: 'Was it good, mother? Was it good?'

'Yes, son,' she whispered, stroking him.

'If it hurts, it's... better?'

'Yes, son…'

'Shall I keep beating you?'

'Yes, son…'

Then they fell silent. He wanted to ask why the tall man didn't beat her, why she didn't ask him to do it. But something stopped him. Maybe he did, he thought. With this hope his loathing for Geder evaporated, to be replaced with something else. When he was drifting off to sleep, Geder assured him that he did beat his mother, that she was happy, and he felt he liked Geder, he even stroked his sleeve…

…then he drifted off completely…

…oblivious…

From then on his mother no longer returned late at night and Janek no longer wandered the woods until dusk. In the evenings they sat inside, eating corn bread or boiled potatoes, speaking quietly, a benign peace between them. They enjoyed watching each other's gestures, the former sense of alienation had gone, they kept meeting each other's eyes and feeling comfort in their closeness. The evenings were still humid and the moon kept shining.

One evening they heard a noise outside and a moment later the door opened. On the threshold stood the enormous figure of old Hudorovec.

They turned to stone.

Janek's mother was poking the fire beneath the pot, Janek was sitting on the bed.

'Home already?' she asked in surprise, still mechanically poking at the fire.

'Home, wife, home!' said the old man. Janek was surprised that he gave 'wife' a strange emphasis. Usually he said 'woman'. And he had never spoken so quietly, coldly, crisply. He put his battered suitcase in the corner. He closed the door behind him. He did everything slowly, pensively. Then he began to unfasten his belt.

'What about you? You're home, too?' he asked, looking at her.

'What do you mean?' his wife whispered.

Her voice was hoarse, it trembled slightly.

'You should be up there, with that one. Eh, wife?'

'What are you saying?'

Hudorovec, meanwhile, had removed his belt and ran it through his open left hand. Then he stretched it in front of his chest, as if testing its strength. He was doing everything coldly, thoughtfully.

'Come here, wife!' he ordered. She froze.

'Out, boy!' He turned to Janek. 'Did you hear me?' he yelled, when Janek failed to move. Now his coolness was gone, his face distorted, saliva flew from his mouth, his eyes glistened.

'Out!' he yelled once more. Then his enormous paw grabbed Janek by the shoulder. As he flung him towards the door, Janek's head struck it so hard he felt dizzy. Again the bony fingers reached for him and the next moment he was outside the door. It closed behind him. He got up, rushed at the nearest pine tree and grabbed hold of it, shaking.

From inside he heard his mother moaning. He could hear the blows of the leather belt. Hudorovec was panting and swearing. It sounded as if he was banging her head against the floor.

'Whore…' he gasped, 'bitch…'

'Stop it, stop it!' pleaded his wife. 'I had no choice, husband… my dear husband! How was I supposed to live, when you go off, not caring whether we die of starvation!'

'You could work, you slut! Take that… and that… And the boy could work…'

'I did, I did…' she insisted, but she was becoming quieter. She cried out a few times, then she was silent. The blows kept falling.

Janek ran off through the woods. On the hill he stopped and watched the trunks of the beech trees trembling with light. He realised it was lightning. There was thunder above the plain, a wind had started up, a storm was coming, the first in quite some time.

Long into the night he was washed by the rain. He turned his cheeks to the sky. He opened his mouth and eyes to feel the falling drops. The treetops were shaking. The flashes of light shimmered, never disappearing.

The priest sat at the open window. He was looking across the valley to the village at the end of the ridge. He had a chilling recognition, for everything that he had planned to think calmly about was revealed in the first moment; but because it was revealed too quickly, he was confused. He felt he would be unable to focus, at least at the beginning, so that the delusions would be fragmented and deceptive.

It had started with the tall chestnut tree above the valley, which was over three centuries old. It was a special thing, not only in appearance, but also in its significance. The wood around it had long ago been cut down, long before the priest came to these parts. Where the trees had been felled there were saplings growing and thick bush. Next to this miniature wood the chestnut seemed even bigger, like a great grandfather or guardian. It could be seen from the other side of the valley and from the north, where the low hills became a higher rise, and even from the plain, from the south, when it was clear. For many years it had been washed by storms and had lost its crown a number of times during turbulent nights. Since the winds blew mainly from the west, over the years it had wearied and leaned crookedly over the valley. It aroused unpleasant feelings, especially on stormy summer nights, when it swayed menacingly before the flashing background. But lightning hadn't struck it for many years.

People created a legend: when the burning hand from the sky shattered the solitary old tree or it was touched by unworthy human hand, then great misfortune would befall the valley. The legend had been woven from one generation to the next. The priest knew that all in the valley paid homage to the tree; they paid for masses to be said in its honour and spoke of it in whispers, cautiously. He also had a strange respect for it himself: whenever he went by he felt a special solemnity and hurried his step. Instead of fading away, the belief strengthened from one generation to the next, for children received it from their parents at that age when they are most open to the miraculous, the fairy-tale. The priest knew that the child's soul is like a freshly ploughed field; when it absorbs faith, it carries it within, without being aware of it, for the rest of its days.

But the monotony of the empty belief had gone on for so long that no one really believed in the prophecy. He had spoken about this quite often with Geder, the tall, skinny farmer, who lived a solitary life on the edge of the village. Then it suddenly happened. It must have been the suddenness of the event that made the priest succumb so excessively to the mysterious premonition. One night, a storm raged above the valley, the like of which hadn't been seen for a long time. It was the first storm of the year: it was barely the end of April and the heavens had opened. The next morning the whole valley was gripped by horror. The previous evening they had seen the sacred chestnut swaying violently on the hill, illuminated by lightning, but the next morning where it should have stood there was only clear blue sky, washed by the storm.

The priest once again looked across the valley and tried to work out whether the sky was really lighter. Of course it was, since it was early morning. He might not have realised what had happened if old Nancashka hadn't rushed into the presbytery, fallen on her knees and sobbed that God had sent a sign and that the centuries-old chestnut tree was no more... It was then he turned and looked out of the window and saw empty sky. He was stunned, the ground felt unsteady beneath his feet. What disturbed him most was that a circle had been broken and he would need to work out what was happening.

'What can you do,' he tried to calm the almost hysterical woman, 'we haven't had such a storm...'

'No, Father!' she almost yelled. 'The chestnut was not uprooted, someone chopped it down! Can you imagine how much effort was involved? Only the devil could have done it!'

And she rushed off, as if the devil really was hot on her heels. The priest was awash with uncertainty; a feeling that continued all that day and all night, and even more so the next morning – a Sunday, when more people flocked to church than he had ever known. He stood in the pulpit. They stared at him, waiting for him to announce a miracle. How much despair flooded his heart, how many lies and doubts awoke in him, how clear it became that things were happening of their own accord, spontaneously, irrationally, far from folks' beliefs and their demands to elevate the trivia! He would prefer to avoid explaining the event, for he did not wish to pretend. He knew that he was in dire need of reflection, that he could say nothing that he would not doubt the next moment. But the people were staring at him, they were all eyes. It struck him that he could not reveal to them the ruin that existed inside him. He began to speak.

'The old chestnut tree,' he said, 'which was and is no longer.'

He was interrupted by a man's voice from the congregation. 'It still is, Father. After the storm it was wreathed in mist and for some time we couldn't see it from the village. It's standing there, where it always has. Go and look.'

The priest saw the staring eyes of the congregation grow even bigger, darker, as if they had alighted on something completely incomprehensible. Almost as if they had expected that the prophecy had come true. He was gripped by waves of despair, he lowered his eyes and right below the pulpit he saw Geder with a scornful look on his unshaven face and blinking eyes that said: You don't believe in God, Father, and nor do these people! Then he hung his head even lower. Again he had the feeling that the ground was unsteady beneath his feet. His legs carried him from the pulpit and in the sacristy he leaned for some time against the cold wall. Eventually, he gathered enough strength to go before the altar and lead mass.

It began after that Sunday. He was increasingly conscious of how much deceptive light there was about him. And the valley, with its superstition, had shown itself to be an empty surface beneath which life followed its own laws and things happened of their own accord. Geder, who visited him a few days later, confirmed his suspicions. When the priest expressed his surprise that the irrational scare among the people had so quickly faded, Geder said that it was natural, for among these people faith, of whatever kind, was like straw: it burned up as soon as it was lit. But if the Church would confirm that the old chestnut tree was sacred, people would begin to panic, for the Church was the law that needed to be followed out of habit. They would have confirmation that what they believed was true, they would have support. But there was no belief among the people, although there was always a widespread conviction that the chestnut tree was an expression of some higher order.

The priest never forgot what he said to Geder.

'You, Geder, are the only one in the valley with your own world and probably even you are not capable of believing in it. You can be reconnected with the world of the people you belong to socially only by an accident that brings together those different worlds. But that which comes unexpectedly, cutting across man's path and intentions comes from one source. If the chestnut really is connected with an evil that may cause harm, then it doesn't matter whether we believe in it or not. For when evil is present, it is impossible to withdraw from it. Faith is thus not important, but rather the evil that is manifested. However, we can console ourselves that the evil that may befall the valley can be foreseen. It will either be a bad harvest, or an accident, or a death. But that is not real evil, that is nature, it's what happens. And if what happens is reality, then evil is something that is not real, because it does not happen in accordance with nature but against nature. The evil that might affect you, Geder, or anyone else in the valley has only one source. When we talk about evil, we must talk about the source of that evil. And that source, Geder?!'

Geder was known to be a freak, in his solitude he read books, he was educated up to a point, but he looked down on the others in the valley. The farmers did not like him. They talked about him, discussed his personal affairs and passed on gossip. At the same time, they were afraid of him, probably because he always behaved in an arrogant fashion, often ignoring them. The priest knew the valley well, he knew that the soul of the farmer was not a complex thing. In every arrogant person the farmer sees something higher, something more powerful and hates the person because he also fears him. The priest knew that Geder was no exception, for there was no one in the valley who liked him. Whoever did something that raised him in the eyes of others became the subject of envy.

In the countryside it was impossible to do anything that elevated you in the eyes of others. Above all, no one should do anything spiritual, whatever it might be. Everything was strictly determined, everything confirmed by ancient customs. If someone came back from Germany, having worked day and night, and distributed among the neighbours some third class rags that he supposedly bought there, he would be talked about everywhere; people would know him, would talk about him at every opportunity, but all would regret they were not in his shoes. It needs to be acknowledged that this man would not be liked at all – quite the opposite: they would not like to see him, for he would remind them of his money and the awareness that this money was not theirs would bring about intolerable suffering! If someone were to criticise something publicly and was bold enough to revolt against the municipal bureaucrats, in other words if he was less cowardly than the others, he would not become a hero in their eyes – he would be a fool. And if the bureaucrats then took their revenge against him, then people would laugh, voicing their satisfaction at the fact that he brought it upon himself.

The priest knew that on the sly, everyone delighted in the misfortunes of those close to them, they were envious of anyone who had a measure of wheat more than them. And he also knew that they had no respect for him. The women brought him gifts, they helped him one way or another, they went to mass, but for them he was just a figure embodying age-old traditions, he wasn't a real person. He always had the feeling that they saw in him something self-evident, as self-evident as the fact that wheat ripens in the summer and not the autumn.

The priest did not contradict Geder's opinion, even though he thought somewhat differently. Or at least, it seemed to him that he thought somewhat differently. At the same time, he often had to acknowledge that he saw the valley in its true colours precisely through Geder's words. He knew the peasant mind, but he never found the courage to condemn it. And if he were to contradict Geder's words, he would have to speak in its defence. But he was incapable of that, for with each year that went by he was more disappointed in his parishioners. The years had made him accustomed, and he had accommodated to the nature of the valley so that his disappointment was not apparent. In Geder's discourse he often felt undertones of guilt, as if with the fury that Geder poured on the valley he was excusing his solitude, which the priest knew was not voluntary, but forced upon him by circumstances. But he did not delve into this, for he feared what might come to the surface; he satisfied himself with shallow conversations that risked nothing.

The farmers who knew that Geder had a low opinion of them defended themselves. You, Geder, they said, you say that we farmers are worth no more than dung, that we are lazy and cowardly. But tell us: are you any different? Or are you perhaps not the worst of all! You always put yourself above us, but who are you, what do you have? Your house is falling down around your ears, we can see that from the valley, you have only one cow and its ribs are sticking out, you buy a pig in the winter for slaughter because you don't have your own, your hens perish, your fields are full of weeds, you are dirty, and yet you look upon us as dung!

The priest knew that much of this was true and yet he often took Geder's part, almost as if he wished to apologise to him for something. Thus he had got used to such thoughts, which he had taken for his own in the firm belief that they grew from his own experience. Perhaps because, by some strange coincidence, Geder always confirmed what had grown in the priest's own heart but dared not come to the surface until supported by Geder's words.

They also talked about faith. Geder said that he did not believe in the God that the priest served up in church.

'It seems to me that there is a God, but not as described by you and the Bible,' he said. 'But in spite of that I think we can talk about faith, or precisely because of that. If I believed in your God, we could deal with this in church, don't you think? But as far as this valley is concerned: are you convinced that all these churchgoers are really believers? A funny question, I know. You would say it was heretical.

But I have an idea – such ideas are called theories, I read that some-where – I have a theory that none of these people believe in God, but they believe more in the habit of believing. They pray and go to church only because that's what their parents and grandparents did, and that's what they do everywhere. These people do not live, Father. These people are because it is the habit that they are and they are what the habit is. I've put it rather oddly, but look… The other day, for a change, I was in church and I watched these people. There were some young lads laughing during your sermon. I'm sorry, but I saw it with my own eyes. And they were eyeing the girls on the other side. The girls were pretending that they didn't know they were being looked at, but they were blushing and I know very well what those girls had on their minds. I'm sorry, maybe it's inappropriate what I'm about to tell you, but what the girls are thinking about in church, no less than the boys, is that thing that I won't talk about now. That's what they're thinking about! For these peasants, Father, are very fond of it. I ask you, where are their thoughts of God?! You would rely most of all on the old ladies who always kneel in the aisle. But let's be honest, why do all these women, old and young alike, go to church? Let me tell you, Father. I had a wife, people say this and that, but you and I know how it was. She used to come to confess to you, but maybe she told you something different to how it was. For a long time, almost to the end, she almost forced me to go to church. I told her I simply didn't believe in God and it would be a sin if I went, but she said… imagine… you believe what you want, but what will people say, everyone goes and you could do what your father used to do, why should you act any different from others? You should see how devoutly Matay stares at the altar, but otherwise he's a savage! I ask you. She was just caught up in a habit. So where does God come into it, and faith? And my wife, Father, that's what the people of this valley are like. They're not people, they are objects that habit plays with and that Habit is your God. And I'll tell you something else: my wife believed in spirits, in witches, in various mysterious signs, in ghosts, in moving lights and so on. That's just superstition, Father, as you well know. I often said to my wife: Listen, you believe in God, so how can you also believe in ghosts and such like, it's heresy! And she said I was a Calvinist, that I was possessed by the devil! You can't explain anything to a person in the grip of Habit, because such a person has no sense or whatever it is. I don't know how to explain that.'

The priest was aroused from his ruminations by the evening chill slipping through the window: he didn't want to close it because he liked perusing the valley. It was wreathed in dusk. He went over to the cupboard and unfolded the confessional robe made from thick, warm material. Then he sat down again, crossed his arms and leaned forward slightly. The valley lay below him. In its way it was coming closer to him. He could think more easily like this. When everything was unclear, everything that disturbed him was revealed.

Besides Geder's, there was one other separate world that defied peasant superstition and that was the world of the gypsies. The priest knew it well since they attended church and came to confession, but in spite of that it had often seemed to him that he knew only their exterior and that he could not penetrate the depths of their character, even if he wanted to. He had read a number of books on this stubborn race that history had broken, trampled on and cheated a hundred times, but never destroyed. Even in those books he did not find the truth, since they were far from the essential nature that he knew and they failed to clarify the incomprehension that hung over the gypsies like a shadow. In their customs and their inability to adapt he saw something ineffable, something that defied thought, explanation; something that simply had to be accepted. He condemned all those who rummaged among the roots of gypsy life in order to somehow erase it, to blend it with peasant or worker's blood. He also condemned those who went so far as to demand the status of national minority for the gypsies. They could not be erased since no one had managed to do so in a thousand years, yet neither could they live as a nation, otherwise they would have become one long ago.

The priest knew the nature of this character, its uniqueness and stubbornness. He knew that the gypsy did not control his own nature, that he constantly undermined himself and his principles. But he did this spontaneously, without evil intent. If he promised to come tomorrow to help with the harvest the promise would be a serious one. But the next day it might happen that he didn't come. If anyone accused him of lying they would be unjust, for when he swore he would come his intention was firm. But since the previous day much had changed. The sun had gone down, the moon had sailed across the sky, the sun had risen again, the wind was blowing… and the gypsy thinks with the weather, he moves in the way that nature moves. His forebears' traditions reach back a thousand years, controlling him and his blood. His actions are dependent on coincidence, on the moment. There is nothing in the world that the gypsy clings to or completes. With the exception of music. Music is a part of the tradition that belongs to his life.

That was how the priest saw the gypsies who lived in his parish.

The inheritance of blood can break through even the most intellectual crust that had been laid over it. That was probably why nothing came of any of the agreements that gypsies had signed with well-meaning men. In the priest's view, in all the attempts to integrate the gypsies there had been too much bureaucracy, too much morality and not enough cunning. After the war they had been moved to Banat and Bačko, given fields and 'a better life had been pressed into their hands.' And what had happened? The nomads had been gripped by homesickness. Not a week went by without them returning to their old homes, as if they had buried treasure concealed in the poor earth. And they said that not even the devil was going to get them away from there. Every attempt to 'civilise' them had ended in failure. In one of the lowland gypsy settlements they had built a public toilet, because of the terrible smell among the houses. And what had happened: two families had knocked some walls down, nailed some boards up and moved in, so that the toilet was no more.

An assortment of strange things would happen that the priest was only too familiar with, even though he had only one small gypsy hamlet in his parish. He thought that hamlet was the most suitable expression since it contained only four homes.

The population, of course, was considerably bigger. How big could not be determined, because most of the inhabitants moved around all the time. Besides which, anyone trying to undertake a census would experience a wealth of difficulties since the hundred or more residents of the hamlet shared only three surnames: Baranja, Horvat and Šarkezi. And what was worse: the men were almost all called Pišta, Karči, Miška and Evgen, and it was almost impossible to find another first name. If most people were not away from home most of the time, then the postman would find himself in great difficulty. Fortunately, there was not a great deal of written correspondence and many of the inhabitants were illiterate. But in spite of this, it was often difficult to know who to hand a letter to if, for instance, it was addressed to Pišta Baranja, there being five or more in the settlement. In such cases the letter would be opened and from the content and signature, they worked out whose it was. The priest had often been there, in the small wood beneath the hill; and with time their past had been revealed to him.

Pišta Baranja had three sons, two of them married, and four daughters, two of them also married. One son and the daughters each had two or three children, four of which had children themselves, and there were always new ones on the way. His brother had also sired a similar brood. As soon as the younger generation reached the age of thirteen, then new kids began to appear. It was like an anthill. The priest often tried to systematically categorise these human ants, but he quickly tired, for the names of the young ones were the same as the names of the old ones. What was more, in the case of many children it was not even clear who they belonged to. If he wanted to get to the bottom of this Sodom and Gomorrah, he would need a two-metre filing cabinet with many drawers, but in the end it would still defeat him. He knew that this confusion of people and names had already defeated at least one judge.

Of course, it was impossible for this mass to cram into four houses, so the buildings were constantly being added to and extended. Pišta Baranja's house had three wings and two of these had smaller offshoots. It was the same in the case of the others. Young and old went into the world for work, but many returned.

In addition to all those who left, there was still a horde that asked farmers for work, went begging or took on casual labour.

The houses were built of wood and mud. The priest still recalled: once, when living conditions become particularly cramped, Ignac Šarkezi decided to build a two-storey house. Everyone was inspired by the idea and they all helped. There was plenty of wood nearby and, of course, mud. So that the construction would not collapse, they fastened it with ropes to three large pine trees, which were supposed to provide stability. A ladder led up to the first floor. But then one day a terrible wind blew, the pines began to sway and the ropes began to pull the house hither and thither. Cracks started to appear and then the house collapsed.

Since then, they had avoided anything so ambitious. But the overcrowding was getting worse. It was not so bad in the summer, when they cooked outside and even slept outside, scattered through the woods, and there was no hunger then: there was always something to do for the farmers, the road was being widened, they did the odd bit of building, dug ditches, picked apples. Most were in Slavonia or Banat doing seasonal work. And there was blessed peace at home. Some wove baskets, made brooms and other objects, which the women then sold around the villages. They bred dogs and sold them, they also cut firewood and again there was work and bread. In the evenings they played their fiddles in village inns and at weekends at celebrations. Sometimes there would be bloody fights, but that was normal, that strengthened the positive atmosphere. In the summer the atmosphere in the gypsy settlement was always at its peak. They knew how to live so intensively, that they never gave the slightest thought to autumn.

But the time came when the sun disappeared and darkness shrouded the valley, rain began to fall and cold crept across the land. Then they all huddled inside, and had to look for shoes, hats and warmer clothes, for there was no work anywhere, doors were closed to them, seasonal workers returned from the four corners of the wind, worn out, deadly weary, and overnight melancholy sneaked into the rooms where the kids clambered over each other, where it was smoky, dirty, sooty; women gave birth in the presence of men and children, and the rain mercilessly poured and found its way through the roof. At such moments, the inhabitants of the hamlet were gripped by an unusual calm, they spoke quietly, but at length and intensively, they hardly went anywhere, children scratched away at fiddles, school age children leafed through dog-eared exercise books. Then winter came, the schoolchildren got the right to shoes so they could get to school and back, while all the others had to hang around in their shacks, packed in like sardines. They sat smoking bad tobacco, patching, knitting, the whole time wondering how to get firewood, how to get cheap clothes and shoes, as well as the odd potato and other things.

At that time three people appeared in the settlement. The man was incredibly big, with a hairy face, hands like bear's paws, with his bulky shape reminiscent of a bear's. On his back he carried three big bundles. He was panting so hard that the air whistled, on his tousled hair he had a torn hat, his eyes were enormous, whitish and bulging, as if they had been stuck to his face. With him were a woman and a very small boy. The woman, too, was loaded down with things. She was good-looking, of medium height and well built, with silvery black hair and eyes. She was probably approaching forty, certainly not more. The boy was probably about thirteen, but could have been older, for his irregular and almost ugly face showed an unusual seriousness. His small, protruding eyes were reminiscent of a grown-up's and sometimes showed a kind of absence; if you were to look into his face for a long time it might make you shudder. The boy was also carrying two full bags on his back.

Everyone gathered outside, since it was unusual for a stranger to appear there and this little group looked particularly interesting. Then the big bear asked who was the 'boss' and they all pointed to Pišta Baranja. The bear announced that they were gypsies from far off, that their name was Hudorovec, that where they had lived until now there were many gypsies named Hudorovec, that they had left because... life there was strange and so on. The bear spoke a foreign dialect that the gypsies could barely understand. They looked at him and did not particularly believe him since this Hudorovec, which is what he claimed to be, did not look at all like a gypsy, for he was as big as an old beech tree and they never grew so big, they were small and skinny and well proportioned, while this one had incredibly long legs and a short torso, and his face was very unusual, long, oval, a bit like a pear. The wife, on the other hand, was clearly one of them, you could see at first glance, and also the boy, if he didn't look quite so strange.

But suddenly Hudorovec began to speak Romany, for he realised no one understood his dialect. Immediately all their faces cleared, and everyone gathered round and shook their hands, for this was a convincing proof: no one but a gypsy could speak Romany, that was crystal clear. Questions began to rain down on them, Pišta Baranja invited them inside, they put down their stuff, one word led to another and Hudorovec said that… if no one had any objections… if it wasn't too much of an imposition… that they might stay here, see how it went and so on. Why not, they all replied, stay, there's room for three, they'd work, the summer wouldn't be so bad, they could make their own house, there was plenty of wood and more than enough mud. And so it ended up that Pišta Baranja let them have some space in the second extension to his house, they put all their stuff there, and they ate with the Baranjas and sometimes with the Horvats.

On the first day young Hudorovec accompanied the other school kids and from then on attended school regularly. Time passed. The community took in Hudorovec as one of their own, for they could see that he was a real gypsy – a little odd in his habits, it was true – but he had lived elsewhere and he would adapt, no problem.

The sun returned, things began to blossom, trees and plants took on a lively green colour, and the first groups of gypsies began to leave the settlement. The Hudorovec family was there, eating with the others in turn, but they didn't do a thing, they just settled in; the boy fought with the little Horvats, Baranjas and Šarkezis, the mother gossiped with the women, while the father was a strange one and spent most of his time wandering through the woods. All three of them had quite an appetite. And then Pišta Baranja called a meeting, a delegation went to Hudorovec and said… we've nothing against you, Hudorovec, you're not in the way, you're a gypsy like us and we'd give you the shirts off our backs… but build yourself a house, we'll help you, and you have a woman to cook for you… it'll be good for you and for us.

And so they rambled on, it was difficult for them to say these things and they would have preferred not to, but they had no choice. They had noticed that there was a difference between them and Hudorovec, that he was very much his own man, and they became uncomfortable, for at these words Hudorovec did very little, they had seriously offended him, he frowned but he did not move, nor did he say anything. They were not prepared for such a reaction, they didn't understand it. Hudorovec felt humiliated. But the others had experienced so many humiliations that they no longer felt new ones, and it was impossible to cause offence amongst them. And now Hudorovec was acting so oddly! It had never occurred to them that they might hurt his feelings, for they had only given him good advice. And yet he was being like this!

After this conversation he stayed quiet for two days, he looked so disgruntled that his eyes bulged even more, he took to sitting in the woods, gasping for breath as if he had asthma or was carrying a heavy load. Then one day he reappeared and called his son. And they proceeded to move all the family's possessions out into the open.

The others stared: 'Hudorovec, what the devil are you playing at, what's wrong with you, man, we're not throwing you out, take those things back inside!' But Hudorovec said not a word and his eyes became sharper and brighter with satisfaction, for this was his idea of revenge. They all saw that the man was stubborn, defiant and that he could not be dealt with in a reasonable way, their way.

Then he produced an axe from somewhere and began to carry it around, so that all the Baranjas, Horvats and Šarkezis could see it, and he did it without a grin, his face oddly distorted. The mother and boy used to sit among the trees the whole time. She would cook something in a pot and the boy would gather firewood. They kept whispering to each other, they spoke to no one else, and the community thought them strange, impossible to understand.

Then one day the sound of an axe being used came from a nearby wood: Hudorovec and his son were cutting down trees. The wood lay below the top of the hill and spread across its slopes into the valley. To the left were some bushes above which stood the gigantic old chestnut tree. When a number of straight trees had been cut down, they moved to the other slope, across the stream and cut their way forward. Every evening they went down from the stand of beech trees, across the meadow and the stream and up into the woods. While the father swung his axe, the boy had to stand guard on the edge of the wood, which belonged to a local farmer, or so the Baranjas and Horvats said. The sound of trees being cut down continued to come from the woods. Then they dragged the timber into the valley, to the stream and beyond it to the settlement. It was hard work. The boy would have collapsed under the weight a hundred times if his father, at the front, had not cursed and threatened that he'd skin him alive if he didn't keep up. The mother did not help, she had fallen ill and was drifting through the trees like a shadow. Finally, when the timber was all in a heap, Hudorovec silently chose a space near the other houses and began building.

Then the Baranjas, Horvats and Šarkezis came and said that they would help, and that they had quite a bit of experience, and they'd do the roof first, and a lot more mud would be needed... and here and there... and this and that... Hudorovec didn't say a word, but they helped and he didn't drive them away. They kneaded the mud, adding wheat husks they had acquired from nearby farms. It wasn't long before the Hudorovec family had a new home.

The priest didn't know exactly when the young Hudorovec began to trouble him. Certainly not until the mother brought him to church. That was when he began to stand out in his mind. But it possibly began before, during conversations with village teachers who spoke with fear of the boy's strange qualities. Although the other schoolchildren reacted with him in a relaxed way, he seemed too taciturn. He was completely different from the other Roma children. They represented a good third of the school and were a special branch on their own. Even their appearance was different from the farmers' children: ragged and dirty, their books and exercise books tatty and creased, they were as careless as you could imagine, although they were clearly bright. They liked getting into fights and were always causing trouble. But from the first day, Hudorovec was a surprise. He was placid, hard-working, different. He came to school in poor, but clean clothes. He gave the impression that he simply didn't care what was happening in school. He never listened and during lessons he stared thoughtfully at the bench in front of him. But whenever the teacher asked him a question he answered quietly, slightly hoarsely, without any awkwardness, and always gave the answer that was expected and sometimes more.

Yet he always spoke coldly, looking at no one, staring into space, as if he saw in front of him nothing but air. The priest's eyes were immediately opened after the first mass that the mother attended, bringing the boy with her. He spoke to Geder about it that very evening and was almost a little excited, which was unusual for him.

'You know, Geder,' he said, 'on Sunday I met the Hudorovec family. Actually, not all of them, the father wasn't there. Her and the boy. And that boy, I tell you… In the presence of the mother I asked him if he sincerely believed in God and he stared at me for a while as if wanting to take a good look at me, and what I felt was akin to horror, because he wasn't really looking at me and didn't see me. Then he suddenly said, very calmly: "I don't know, Father". I was stunned by his honest reply. When I chatted with him I realised that this child – for he's still really a child – lives in a strange state of obsession, which he clearly cannot grasp rationally, or else is afraid of. He reminded me of someone who is about to act, but still does not know whether he will do so or not. And I get the impression that he does not know what the action should be. He looks as if he is caught up in this tension, this suffering! If you could see his face! Take a look at him some time, look in his eyes and you'll see a kind of disgust, as if he has been completely shocked by something. And yet when he stares like that into the distance, his eyes almost glow, as if he is longing for something beautiful. To say that the boy is torn would not fully describe it, since it's not that simple. And listen: evidently he's the best pupil in the school. I asked him what the teachers were like, how they got on and he said: "I give them the answers they want to hear". I looked at him in disbelief: "Surely you answer what you think is right, don't you?" And after a while he shakes his head. "Why ever not?" I asked him. Now he replied very decisively: "What they say does not come from them, but from elsewhere, and it seems to me that what they don't know is different… They scare me. I want that other thing, what I call theirs, even though it scares me…" That's roughly what he said, Geder. I couldn't repeat his exact words, I was a bit shaken. But imagine! The child seems intelligent, but Geder, I'll say this only to you: I get the impression that he's not quite right. A strange child, strange and mistrustful. That also worries me, Geder, because you never know when it might grow into something sinister.'

It was the last day of May. Young Hudorovec was sitting on the hill and looking at the land below. He was crouching on the grassy edge of the fields that sloped down towards the valley and among which were houses, vineyards and orchards. He could see the plain all the way to the horizon, but on the right the outline of the mountains was very hazy because of the mist; you could see them properly only when the air was very clear. On the plain were villages, woods and fields; far away were two bell towers, indicating a small town. He liked these strange places very much, for where he had lived until now everything was very different. For quite some time he had enjoyed coming up here in the evenings, to get away from the settlement. As soon as he got accustomed to the idea that the distant horizon was new to him and in his mind he began to seek other new things, then his thoughts strayed to the past of their own accord and images, events, faces appeared before him.

Where he grew up there was no plain, there were hills everywhere, although not so high, and when you climbed to the top of one you saw more of the same. There, the view was always interrupted. Here, when he looked into the distance nothing disturbed his view.

You could see where the earth met the sky. He soon noticed something interesting about this; when they first came to the plain his mother said that the people there, whenever they were thinking about something, looked straight in front of them as if staring into the distance; but in their old home, when people were thinking, they looked down, or even up at the sky, as if they couldn't see into the distance and this had become part of their habits.

This was the first thing that gave him pleasure: that he could look ahead and see no end in front of him. He quite enjoyed staring into space. Everyone said he thought too much. Now, when there was no longer any barrier before him, the images in his mind became denser, more visible – as if they had come closer. Sometimes he reached out his hand, because he had the feeling that he could touch everything that he could see in front of him. He felt relaxed in some way, whereas where he'd lived before everything felt more cramped. Of course, he never thought about this fully consciously. It was just a feeling flowing in his veins. The new world had possessed him so completely that past events, even though not all that remote, seemed wreathed in mist. Although his thoughts often strayed to the past there was quite a bit of effort involved, he had to try hard to extract the image from the mist. When he looked more clearly he saw that it wasn't actually mist, but rather traces of this new world obscuring the images from the past. It was as if the new world was preventing him from looking at the past. But this was again only a surface appearance that he could barely penetrate. It wasn't the new world that was holding him back, but he himself, unwilling as he was to return to the anxiety of the past. He was not clearly aware of any of this. But within him floated an uncertain awareness that there must be something in the past that he was afraid of and wished to save himself from. For on remembering the past he felt anxious, whereas as soon as was submerged in his new environment he felt a relaxed sense of joy.

But the more he tried to suppress the past with the new world, the more he actually uncovered it, or it revealed itself to him, for in spite of the fear of anxiety, there was a desire for it somewhere inside him, probably because it wasn't merely anxiety, but was mixed with longing. He noticed that in this new environment it wasn't only him who changed, but also his mother. In a special way, she distanced herself from him; it felt as if she was no longer near. She was like a performance in front of him, but one that tormented him with a physical closeness that he no longer perceived. His father, on the other hand, had not changed at all; he still saw him as a rough body right beside him, he could smell his sweat, his words rang in his ears like hammer blows, his laugh was just like it was in the old place.

There had been no settlement in the old place: they had lived in a ramshackle house in the woods and the nearest gypsy family was five kilometres away. Below the wood was a village. The village children chased him, threw stones, called him 'smelly gypo' and accused him and his family of stealing things. He didn't like going into the village, he only went to church, as he had been taught, and to school. Otherwise he wandered through the woods, saying little, growing up solitary and wild. He had a sister who was two years older than him; she was different, she enjoyed meeting up with the village rascals, she was mean and rude, she beat him as much as their father, who had the habit of responding to every little thing with the flat of his hand. In such moments his mother was the only one who defended him, he always ran to her and cried. It seemed that she loved him much more than the others. Sometimes, like an animal, she resisted Hudorovec's violence, putting herself in between them so that the blows rained down on her. The father and sister were allies and were often absent. His mother was the one who had to go from house to house with her basket, begging; she was the one who had to humbly grit her teeth when people made fun of her, or shut the door in her face, or if the children followed her along the road, yelling; she had to cook, fetch firewood, look after the house, their clothes. But when her husband and daughter returned, she was insulted, scorned, beaten. Hudorovec had an old nag that he rode around, he often met with untrustworthy people and got involved with strange goings on, sometimes he was even absent for long periods and children teased the mother that her man was dead and buried. All the money he gained simply disappeared; what he didn't drink, he lost at cards or squandered it in some other way. No one in the family ever knew what he was up to or where.

Young Hudorovec devoted all his thoughts and every step to his mother; he lived with her, suffered with her. He regarded his father and sister with repugnance and fear, but he never revolted, he never tried to run away from this hopeless situation. He was calm and quiet, he obeyed every word of his tormentors. He was somehow convinced that this was the only possible state, for he knew nothing else and so could not long for it. For years things had remained unchanged, at least as far as he remembered, and his relationship with his mother was always the same. She never complained about her husband or daughter, they never even spoke about it, it simply happened and seemed to him self-evident, just as he did not think about his relationship with his mother, but simply lived and felt it.

Things began to shift when he started to leave boyhood behind, around the age of twelve. Perhaps similar things had happened before, but he had perceived them differently or been indifferent to them – he wasn't sure. It was a single incident that helped him to realise that he had long lived in a reality that he didn't know. He used to return from school by the same path that left the road and cut across the fields towards the woods. The path turned and ran along the edge of the trees to a copse that stood alone among the fields, before finally entering the woods. He had once seen his sister in the copse with three lads from the village; they were perhaps a year or two older than her. He had hidden behind a bush and watched. The youths were trying to convince her of something, then she spoke and held out her hand, they each gave her something, but from that distance he couldn't see what. Then his sister reached for her waist, lowered her skirt, stepped out of it and, naked from the waist down, lay on the ground. Then the largest lad undid his trousers and lay between her legs, while the other two watched.

At this point his memory was fainter and all he remembered clearly was that he stared at the scene for some time, then leaped up and ran home as fast as he could in tears, into his mother's arms. 'What is it? What is she doing?' he sobbed out. His mother was frightened and stared at him. 'What don't you understand?' she finally said. She was surprised, for usually it was unnecessary to explain these things to gypsy children. But young Hudorovec did not know, he had grown up more or less alone, in the woods, and had never spent much time with the other kids. His mother was no less scared than he was, she tried to find the right words, but they would not come, since she never spoke much and certainly not about such things. She explained to him in different ways that everyone did this, even his father and mother and, it seemed, his sister, for she was already fifteen years old, and he would also... 'Why? Why?' his eyes beseeched her. 'How do I know!' she said, staring at him. 'It's just nice, it can be pleasant. I was still little when I found out about it, so how come you don't know?'

His mother couldn't get over her surprise. And for him a new era began. When his sister returned home, he looked at her with new eyes, in fact he looked at everyone differently. Between him and his mother an unusual relationship developed, a kind of embarrassment, with each feeling guilty in front of the other. He started to observe his sister's body, which hitherto had not excited him at all. He saw it was different from his. But the strangest thing of all was that the image of his sister was soon replaced by his mother's. He clung to his mother's body with curiosity. And a fear that he did not understand entered his feelings for her. It appeared often, confusing him.

There was only one room in the house, where all four slept on straw mattresses. Most often there were only three of them, since Hudorovec was often absent. In the corner hung a cauldron for cooking, beside it a wooden bench with scratched pots and pans, while in every corner there were heaps of rags and firewood. On one occasion, old Hudorovec returned late at night. Outside he could be heard talking to his weary nag, then he fell through the door, tripped and staggered drunkenly. He collapsed onto the bed, which was covered with old sacks. It was dark in the house, so young Hudorovec saw nothing of what happened that night, only heard. He lay in the corner on his bed without moving.

His father wheezed, dusted himself down, even tried to sing; he grumbled a bit, then fell silent as if listening to something. All that could be heard was a subdued panting. Then it seemed that the father got up, fell over and at the same moment the mother yelped: 'Ow, that's my stomach... you're suffocating me.' Her husband kneaded and panted and rambled on: 'You're my woman, you get it... I can have you whenever I want... where is it...' and he coughed in between. 'Clothes off... off, I said!... that's it... leg here... that's right... you see, you're a good woman... damn it...' he coughed again.

Then he fell silent and for a long time only heavy breathing could be heard. Now and then he coughed and said something unrecognisable. Then his wife gave a suppressed sigh, the straw rustled and finally there was complete silence. Her husband rolled over. 'Hahaha!' he tried to laugh, but only a kind of gargling emerged. He sighed. Then he suddenly shouted: 'Where's the other woman? Where are you, women are only good for one thing!' He struggled over to his daughter, who lay opposite him. 'Ha, you're already a woman as well... you know how to do it, you do it with others, now it's my turn...!' then laughter burst from him, as he felt around among the straw. Then his daughter also laughed, as if she was being tickled and the father said: 'Hey, you're better than your mother... take it and stick it in, so I don't have to try so hard...' After that the movement and the growling began again.

Young Hudorovec half sat against the wall of the house, holding his breath as feelings of horror washed over him. It was not simply horror, much else was mixed in; and this confusion boiled inside him, bubbling like rising waters that threaten to overflow their banks at any moment. He was to experience this feeling often, every time the same. This was not fear of something terrible, like man's fear of death, or ghosts, or the dark, it was something else, but even later, when he thought about it rationally, he was unable to identify or define the nature of this feeling. It was the horror of awakening, the torment of recognition, full of unknown delights and almost yelling out loud, as if the boy had spotted a snake in front of him that both frightened him and filled him with hope. Yet it was not ordinary fright, for he did not know yet that it was a snake, no one had taught him he could be bitten, no one had taught him he should be afraid. The fear was evoked by the monstrous nature of this unknown creature that was hissing in his face; fear was evoked by its beautiful, sinuous body; but the fear was also mixed with curiosity about what kind of creature it was and why in his longing for it he was afraid. A desire to get to know the snake arose within him, to become familiar with it and thus quell his horror at the fear he could not understand.

He was unaware of the danger that lay in wait for him: that he would not be able to become accustomed to the snake. That the incomprehensible fear of it would grow and that he would therefore want to kill it.

He stayed awake the whole of that night. Confused thoughts scurried through his brain like ants. The next morning his mother was silent in his presence, his father disappeared early on his horse, while his sister wandered through the house as quietly and apathetically as usual. Then she covered herself with a sack, for it was raining, and went into the village. He crouched in the corner for a long time without speaking, but some force kept raising his eyes towards his mother. He wanted to find some sort of consolation there, some clarification and comfort. But at the same time he was gripped by fear, for after what had happened during the night he feared her presence. Each of her movements was an incomprehensible torment to him. In the end, he couldn't take it anymore, he rushed out the door and headed for the woods. 'Janek, Janek!' she called after him. He hesitated for a moment, he wanted to go back, but then she called again and the fear reappeared, so he ran on without replying.

Later, he remembered only indeterminate shades of his delirium. For quite some time he ran blindly among the trees and the rain poured down on him, then he leaned against the trunk of a leafy old beech tree and caught his breath. Once more he was driven onwards, across meadows and back again, seeking some kind of refuge, convinced he was seeking shelter from the rain. Eventually he found a hollow tree and crept inside. Then it was clear to him that it was not the rain that was troubling him. Again he rushed into the woods and ran. Finally, towards evening, soaked to the skin and breathless, he returned to the house and threw himself down, like a deer hiding in the bushes from its pursuers. His mother pulled him towards the fire. She pushed some hot concoction into his hands. He saw everything as if in a mist. He pushed her hands away.

'Mother!' he managed to say at last, 'was that nice? Was that pleasant? What happened last night?' His mother saw that his eyes were like two coals, his unattractive face was twisted, he was trembling and his posture radiated expectation, as if he was desperate for an immediate explanation. She did not reply, she offered him more of the drink, but he impatiently pushed her hand away and sharply repeated the same words.

Now she began to twist and turn in her embarrassment, but it seemed she had misunderstood the reason for his distress. 'That with your sister, you know...' her voice trembled, 'I don't know... I'm saying nothing, let them do what they want... you must never judge her...' He interrupted her impatiently: 'Not my sister, not her, you! Was that nice, was that pleasant, what you do... you?!' His anger frightened her.

'Your father is after all my husband, we've been doing that for a long time! Everyone does it. There's nothing ugly about it. Without that, Janek, you wouldn't be here! Oh, Janek... you'll see, you'll see...'

Her voice broke, she shook strangely, then she was racked by tears, she sank to the floor and sobbed bitterly. Janek sat by the fire, his eyes blank, as if he was looking inside himself. They stayed like that the whole night. Her sobbing, him staring into space.

Meanwhile, the fire went out.

t rained for a long time. Then winter came. Janek could not remember the winter days clearly, for they blended into one another. The things that went on around him only half roused him from his torpor. The snow was already melting and a warm wind was breathing through the woods when one day Hudorovec arrived on his nag, rushed into the house, looked for something among the rags in the corner, but then, as if finding nothing, left again without a word. A slight rain started to fall. Night came and it was as dark as the end of the world. The other three were sitting silently by the fire, when suddenly it was lighter and there was a crackling noise: the house was on fire. They jumped up and threw things outside. The rotten wood was suddenly in flames, the house collapsed, the beams creaked, soon it was all reduced to a charred heap and the flames subsided. It took less than fifteen minutes for it to be reduced to ash, and all that was left was the odd metal dish that they had failed to rescue. They stared wordlessly at the burnt remains. The rain was falling ever more heavily, a cold wind sprung up, the treetops rustled. The wood had not caught fire because the flames were not high and there was no tree close to the house.

As they stood there in shock it began to sink in that they no longer had a roof over their heads. It was then that the old nag clip-clopped onto the scene, and Hudorovec jumped down and stared at the remnants of the fire. The glowing embers of the beams lit up his face, which was strangely serious and dark. When he spoke in a hoarse voice, he did not move an inch but continued staring at what was in front of him. 'There's nothing left,' he said. 'We'll leave! This is no place for us, gypsies elsewhere live better. We'll go looking for them!' For a moment he was silent, as if thinking things through, and then he said sharply: 'Make a bundle of what's left, load the mare and let's go. Tonight, now, immediately!' He spat out these final words separately. Then he disappeared into the darkness.

When morning came they were already far away. The rain was still falling. They headed north, but kept turning more towards the north-east. The father went first, leading the laden nag, followed by his daughter, the mother and finally Janek. Each of them had a bundle over their shoulder. They didn't speak much; Hudorovec was the only one who knew where they were going, the others felt they were being led blind, for the whole time they travelled through woods, across meadows, through remote villages, so that they were seen by very few people. Janek was at first stunned by the sudden change, but soon he had the feeling that the journey was bringing him a kind of relief. Movement, new places, all this had a calming influence on him. The rain eventually stopped, the sun shone, a warm wind sprung up from the south, spring was relentlessly drawing near. Sometimes they followed field tracks and saw snowy peaks in the distance and everywhere was the babble of water and a feeling of freshness. They slept in the open, they ate what they could beg, but for the horse they got nothing and day by day the already skinny nag's ribs began to show more prominently; eventually, it staggered, fell into the mud with its load, wheezed a few times and expired.

They left it by the path, removed their stuff and went on. They spoke increasingly less. 'A few more days and we're there,' Hudorovec muttered every half hour or so, but even he was barely moving forward, he was so exhausted. At one point Janek began to develop a hacking cough, although it soon subsided. Then the sister's face began to turn yellow and she was gripped by a fever. They asked at houses for her to be taken in but everywhere the door was closed mistrustfully in their faces. They went more slowly. At times they had to hold her up. One day the father said they'd head for a settlement in a nearby valley. There was a train station there. Hudorovec produced some money, bought tickets and they dragged their bundles into the dirty carriage. The train rattled slowly along. They left the hills behind and crossed the plain.

Janek watched with fascination, he had never seen a plain before. The train slowly crossed a wide river; it was greyish, flowing quickly, foaming here and there. Then he sank back into a kind of torpor. All he remembered was getting out at a small town with very wide roads. Then they left the town and headed for distant hills. Hudorovec spoke to a number of people on the road and finally they arrived at a village where there were only gypsies. There his sister was given a bed and warm soup, but although she gulped it down she no longer made a sound, but lay there pale and motionless. Hudorovec asked the gypsies to bury her, for they had just had a death of their own, and to register it where necessary, then he spoke quietly with them and they pointed to the north, towards the hills, and the three survivors carried on.

They arrived at a valley among low hills, and on the slope, in a gypsy settlement, they stopped. Later, Janek often wondered why he remembered the long journey so hazily, why everything was shrouded in a mist of emotions that were not that different from what went before, except that there was a little hope mixed in; he had a feeling that the air was fresher, that it was easier to breathe, his eyes sought new objects and his mind focused on those. Thus he forgot his anxiety, which withdrew into a dark corner of his subconscious.

Towards the end of May the settlement where they had made their home suddenly emptied. People left in droves. After a few days there was peace and quiet. At home remained the old men, a few women, school kids and a few toddlers. Even old Pišta Baranja stayed behind this time, he had rheumatism or something, and even though he tried as hard as he could to get up and go, he couldn't even stand on his own, and they had to hold him up. That winter he had aged terribly, his face was more lined and his skin yellowish, his hands had begun to shake and his cunning eyes were cloudy. So he lay around, warmed himself in the sun and massaged himself with oil, the whole time coughing and spitting.

But Hudorovec did go, unexpectedly. He revealed his decision to his wife and son on the evening of his departure. He had been advised to go instead of Pišta Baranja and take over his workplace as a woodcutter in Slavonia. When he left, he said only 'goodbye' to the neighbours and nothing to his wife and son. They did not look into each other's eyes, they did not offer each other their hands, although handshaking was the habit among the gypsies. They said their goodbyes coldly, but for the first time Janek felt that his father's departure filled him with a strange optimism, his throat felt tight, the seed of a sudden whoop appeared there, but did not develop, it remained inside him and all day he had the feeling that he wanted to laugh out loud. His mother said nothing for quite some time, she kept busy around the house and outside it, she looked furtive and her eyes were oddly bright.

In addition to the old men and children, Emma, the wife of Evgen Baranja, the third son of old Pišta, also stayed behind. She was a young, beautiful woman, around twenty years old, but on the very day of departure she fell ill with stomach cramps, groaning and rolling around on the bed. Her husband stood beside her and tried to persuade her to set off, saying the illness would subside on the journey and that she would have nothing to do if she stayed behind. But she was adamant. Her husband lost his temper, cursed her, grabbed his wooden suitcase and stormed off. Janek noticed that soon after the seasonal workers had departed she stopped groaning surprisingly quickly. She came to the edge of the woods, stood close to him and together they looked down into the valley. Below, beside the stream, a black column of the departing was winding its way across the meadows, with children skipping around, for some had decided to take their whole family, towards the south and the plain. The sun shone down on them. They made their way past a stand of alders and then disappeared among the trees.

'They've gone,' said Emma, turning towards him. He kept looking straight ahead, but could feel her eyes on him.

'Why didn't you go?' he asked, using the formal mode of address, but he immediately regretted it. His voice sounded accusatory.

'Why are you being so formal?' she asked in surprise. 'I'm still young, aren't I?'

He did not reply. He was afraid that his tone of voice would reveal his suspicions: that she was not ill, that she had pretended because she wanted to stay behind. And as if reading his thoughts, after a brief silence she said:

'I wanted to stay here. It's my business, but I'm telling you anyway. In any case, we'll find some kind of work here. What will you do now there's no school?'

'Why are you asking, what do I know?' he suddenly snapped, although he hadn't intended to. In a moment, he felt so embarrassed that without a word he turned and ran towards the house. He was confused by her strange curiosity, but he understood even less his own brusqueness. When he thought about it later, it struck him that until now no one had asked him anything in such an open way, no one had asked him out of the blue what he intended to do. But all that he was thinking about were excuses and finally he admitted that to himself. He knew all too well that in those moments when they stood at the edge of the woods watching the departing seasonal workers, something had taken place. When he had looked at her for a moment, he noticed that she had raised her left hand and was scratching her head – her cardigan was torn underneath her arm and the whiteness of her breast flashed before his eyes. This was only a momentary realisation, because then she lowered her hand, but in that instant it came to him that she, too, did that thing… And with that he felt unease at her proximity, he became curt, until the feeling grew to such an extent that he felt he had to flee.

When Emma later returned to the settlement, he hid in the house and watched through the window. She did not look back, but went straight to the extension of Baranja's house and soon reappeared with a basket, then set off through the wood towards the hilltop, probably to the village. He felt a sense of relief, the tension flowed away. When he came outside he felt he could breathe more easily, that the strange unease had gone, but for the first time in his new environment his old anxiety returned with such speed that he could do nothing to escape it.

Janek's mother began to go frequently to the village, taking on farm work. Most often she was seen at Geder's place. The farmers liked to hire her because she was unbelievably quiet: unlike the other chattering gypsy women, she seemed reserved, even humble, and she worked well, carefully, almost eagerly. She brought various things home to eat, but only in the evening. In the afternoon, when Janek came back from school, the other kids disappeared to the fields and woods. Then he was completely alone. The settlement was silent and empty, the sun shining down on it, and higher up, above his house,

Pišta Baranja sat on the roots of an old beech, puffing on his pipe, beside him lazily stretched out his black and white dog, whose name was Shubi. Now and then a damp breeze blew through the trees, shaking the branches, and from the stream in the valley came the yells of children at play. At such moments Janek felt that anxiety was very near. The objects around him changed form, transformed into things that reminded him of something he had once experienced. If he closed his eyes to defend himself against the associations, in his imagination there began to grow new objects which reminded him of where his anxiety had sprung from.

After the dry, hot sunshine a wet period set in that was reminiscent of spring. What Janek noticed most or almost exclusively were changes to the weather. The atmosphere affected his every move and he treated it the way you would a blanket. Along with the weather, the structure of his feelings changed. With the wet weather he felt as if a south wind was blowing inside him, something thawed, became softer, juices flowed from the depths and circulated through his veins. When he lay in the long grass by the stream, he was often aware of the air above him, of the wind, the waving grass, the buzzing of bees. Of course, the weather was not completely spring-like since it was July, but the pleasant coolness, the freshness of the earth and the wind, were reminiscent of that season. It was summer, but Janek wanted to feel spring and its freshness, and because that was so, that's what he felt. As often before, his senses latched onto nature and drank it in, thus suppressing the thoughts seething inside him. His mind kept reviving various memories, making him relive old events, usually in a revised form; some nuances became more intense, stronger, others were shrouded in mist.

But the movement of nature did not flood him so thoroughly that certain objects did not protrude from the dark surface. One in particular became ever sharper. It had the shape of an axe. When he became almost convinced that it was not an axe, it appeared in front of him in a very distinct way. It floated in the air at different heights, it came closer and receded, sometimes the blade was towards him, then the blunt edge replaced it. The sudden presence of the axe seemed odd to Janek, since he had no memory involving an axe, he saw it merely as an object, not as a part of some previous events. At certain moments it hung right in front of his eyes, so clear that he could see the blunt edge of the blade and the colour of the steel, which was light near the cutting edge and darker at the top. Then, when the image had disintegrated a number of times, it began to trouble him that the bothersome axe kept reappearing before his eyes, as if demanding an explanation for its presence. It kept assailing him for so long that associations began to spring up. They were not connected in any way, merely flashes.

In the end, he felt he had no choice but to succumb. The scene of the storm when he and his father had been cutting down trees to build the house appeared. On that occasion the axe had danced before his eyes for hours and no doubt imprinted itself on his retina. With this realisation he felt relief and the axe disappeared. But it soon returned, as if unsatisfied with the explanation of its presence, as if it was demanding more, and this forcefulness aroused fear in Janek, while at the same time lessening his resistance to the associations that were assailing him. The dike weakened and a swarm of memories splashed across it. Because it happened so suddenly, it was seething and unclear. But certain shades were clearly discernible. The axe no longer hovered in the air, it was hanging on a nail on the wall of the house. Beside it shimmered the bed by the door that his father was supposed to lie on... then his silent footsteps, the swing of the axe... or did he swing it? But the bed was empty... the axe struck nothing... there were only rags and old sacks... so then it was nothing... it was only an intention... or wish... or a recognition that it would be a good thing to do... sometime... in the future. It hadn't actually happened.

He was flooded with an unfamiliar sense of joy – like a man who has seen an apparition before him and then discovered it is only a tree. Now the memories drifted in a relaxed way towards each other, came together, arranged themselves in a sensible order and then once more flowed through him. After that evening when his father had returned and beaten his mother, the idea was born within him that mother was happy when father beat her. But he had been surprised by her gasping, crying, suffering. Long into the night he clung to a tree and was washed by the rain. He thought about everything, new feelings bubbled up within, the horizon became lighter, closer, the sense that he could make decisions grew within him. Of course, he did not realise that his new knowledge was not strong enough to shake his existing attitude towards his mother. That reached its peak when he began to respect Geder, because he assumed that he beat her when they had sex. Then he began to worship and respect everything that brought his mother joy, everything that gave her pleasure, and to hate everything that brought her disappointment and suffering. But there was still one thing he could not understand: why she seemed to enjoy some blows and not others.

The puzzle was solved the next morning by his mother. 'Janek,' she said, with a benign look, 'you are a child and will always remain a child who understands nothing. If someone beats me, it is nice only if he loves me… If someone who hates and wishes to punish me beats me, then it hurts… it hurts terribly…'

The difference thus took on sharp edges, two colours appeared that had no intermediate shades. And his attitude to his mother became the basic outline of his inner world. Between these two poles there appeared and disappeared all his other feelings, it became a physiological law that subjugated his instincts, subjugated his nerves, and redirected them parallel with its strength. The cause of his inner tension was his mother, for she was the only palpable object in the incomprehensibility that he surrendered to out of fear and the desire to overcome it. In these moments Janek's inner world was highly complex and ephemeral, constantly changing shape. This was undoubtedly because a kind of disgust was growing within him for anything that brought his mother suffering. This filled him with extreme hatred for his father.

But it had not happened. The axe stayed on the nail by the door. He ran outside, into the woods, to the earth, the trees, the air, the sky. In the face of his inner confusion he always latched onto nature, which saved him. Once again there was a storm: he didn't know how it had arisen so suddenly, it seemed recently that storms were coming ever more often, as if the sky was making amends for the previous drought. It crashed and crackled, it swept across the valley into the distance, the lightning fading, the darkness creeping in behind it and swathing the diminished woods. It felt as if the storm was passing through him, washing him, and with the final flashes that were already beyond the hills, the spasms of pain inside him also passed. Now he floated, he was empty but fresh, like the air is fresh and empty after a storm.

His father was no longer there, he had vanished, his mother said he'd gone for good, following his own path, and rightly so, she said. He was happy his father had gone, but at the same time he grieved for him, for his mother's tormentor had thus become more distant. And the urge to destroy him had not subsided within him. But in spite of that, now, when he recalled everything, at least one thing was clear: the action had not been carried out, the intention had not been realised. He felt a kind of freedom, a double freedom: he felt his mother's relief and he felt joy because nothing had happened. Because everything had remained as it was before, he felt almost happy that he had not done what he intended.

When the memories trickled away, he began once again returning to nature, to the valley, to things. The grass by the stream had not been cut and was standing high above him as he lay, the grass blades waving in the southerly and swaying past him, now and then one tickling his cheek. The wind also blew through the alders by the stream, making them rustle. The stream bed was now full of water. Higher up, on the steep slope, young beech trees gave way to chestnuts and spruces with the occasional birch; they reached to the ridge and across it, spreading to the south further than he could see. On the other side, on the hill, was the village just above the gypsy settlement. On the slopes to the north and south were fields of wheat and stubble. The wind sometimes carried from there the sound of laughter or the piercing song of a blackbird. He felt satiated, at peace, satisfied.

Something suddenly stirred him, he felt that someone was close, crouching in the grass. He turned his head, raised himself on his hands and opened his mouth. Emma was in front of him, laughing. The awareness of her closeness banished the previous sense of victory. Once again he shuddered.

He never thought about Emma, but whenever he saw her he felt paralysed. Once he tried to connect this feeling to an unusual incident, and remembered once walking up towards the village and seeing an animal lying in a nearby field. He could not make out what it was and this led him to draw nearer to find out. But he was annoyed that this would delay him, since he wanted to be in the village as soon as possible. But although he felt like going over to the animal, he resisted the impulse, since it would divert him from the direct path. And the whole time he also felt afraid that he would find out what kind of animal it was. This was a step he did not want to risk. But then, when he went forward with mixed feelings, he suddenly turned, convinced that he had seen Emma in the fields. A moment later he wondered how he could think something like that!

Her behaviour seemed very intrusive, although it may not have been so. He had the feeling she wanted to take him somewhere he didn't want to go, so he struggled not to think about her and avoided her presence. Of course, he didn't realise that he wasn't struggling against her and her presence, but against his own burning desire to be near to her. This desire sneaked to the front of his mind and lay in ambush for him. Now, when he saw Emma beside him, he burned with a confused mass of feelings. He could clearly recognise the flames of joy and it was this joy that scared him most, so that he froze and wished to flee. He thought she was bothersome, that she was stalking him and gave him no peace, but he was paralysed; although he was convinced he had already reached a decision, his body would not obey him. More confusion flowed through him. When it subsided, he was left helpless and resigned, without will, nature once again collided with him, his mind became cloudy.

Emma laughed. She flicked her wet hands at his face. She had been by the stream, and the hem of her skirt was wet.

'You've been lying there a long time!' she said. 'I saw you from higher up. I thought you were asleep. Or dead!'

She sank to her knees and rested her round behind on her bare feet. Janek looked at her without replying. He unwillingly asked himself where she had seen him from, for he had been lying in the long grass. Maybe she had been on the other hill, above the stream, in the wood. But he didn't ask, for he felt his voice would be strange and would scare him even more. As if reading his thoughts, she said:

'We were harvesting up there!' and she pointed to the hill above the stream. 'I saw you run down here ages ago and then lie down. And when I came down I saw you. I washed my feet in the stream and I'll dry them here. The sun's nice here and no one can see.'

She leaned back on her elbows, her legs slightly bent at the knees, then she pulled her wet skirt to the top of her thighs. Her brown skin held drops of moisture that the sun began to soak up. Her head sank into the long grass and she watched him from there. He turned to the left, towards the settlement. He thought he could hear Šubi barking. Examining the path that led upwards, he felt sure that he could quickly run up it, but he felt a tingling in his limbs, as if he was being pricked with hot needles, and his eyes once again slid towards Emma and he saw that her skirt was now round her waist, almost above her navel, and that she had unbuttoned her thin blouse. The skirt and blouse were all that she was wearing. The tingling flowed to the end of his toes, he felt it in his scalp; the sensations sometimes crawled slowly, at other times seemed to be racing round his body. Her skin was bronzed by the sun, it was firmer than his mother's; he could feel something different in her, with her raven black hair. Her legs were slightly apart and open to the sun, he could see the curve of her pudenda, drops of moisture glistened in the tousled black hair; she was slightly swaying her knees and her gaze held his. He had never seen his mother naked in daylight, he had never seen a woman's sex before, The tingling changed into larger shockwaves...

'Janek, will you bring me a little water from the stream,' she said with a careless, sleepy voice, 'in your hands and pour it on me...'

An invisible force pulled him to his feet and took him to the stream, where he dipped his hands in the water, cupped them and came back. Now she was stark naked, the blouse and skirt had gone. 'Here, pour it on my stomach...' she pointed.

He knelt beside her and poured the water on her navel; there wasn't much, as most of it had escaped from his hands: small trickles ran down the curve of her stomach, she inhaled so that the curve grew more pronounced... 'Massage me a little with the water, with your hand...'

His hand slid down her wet stomach, she took hold of it and pulled it down further, to her sex. 'Here, a little,' she said... He held his hand between her legs, while she raised herself on her right arm. 'Will you do it to me, Janek...' she whispered, 'I'd like you to. Get undressed...'

She helped him, his shirt flew into the grass, she pulled his trousers down, grabbed his penis and squeezed it: her hand was hot, he lay on her, and she placed his right hand on her left breast, the left behind her neck... 'You need to squeeze here...'

She was a big woman, bigger than his mother, his thin body melted between her hot thighs, the tingling was replaced by tongues of flame, the fire was roaring; and then, when he became dizzy, she shoved him away.

'Wait, I haven't said you can yet!' she said harshly.

He lay in the grass. The blood had rushed to his face and he felt tears in his eyes. He was licked by flames, but the astonishment had started to douse them.

'If you want to do it to me, there's something you have to do for me first.' Her voice was brusque, commanding.

He shoved his face into the grass, overcome with dark despair, a sudden bitterness appeared, but soon changed into humility. He felt her hand on his naked back.

'This evening, wait for me at the edge of the woods. I'll tell you what you have to do.'

He heard her slipping her clothes on. Then beating grass from her skirt. Then she walked off. 'Get dressed, in case anyone comes,' he heard her say when she was already a few steps away. The grass was calm beneath her feet.

He leapt up, hurriedly put on his shirt and trousers, and once more threw himself on the ground and buried his face. Tears poured from his eyes and he was shaken by sobbing. He felt he had taken the step that he had so feared, that he had not successfully defended himself and that he was being assailed by things he could not grasp. Emma was new; she came after his mother. And she was different. Although he guessed that relations between them would be like that between him and his mother, he still felt a difference, and that difference filled him with horror. The relationship between him and his mother was the basis of it all, he went to her to calm his fear of what he didn't understand, in her hands he felt safe, because she kept showing him that it was pleasant, that there was nothing to fear… Although he felt no pleasure, but only indescribable horror at the act itself, he was convinced that he was sacrificing himself for his mother's pleasure out of his gratitude to her. But now that feeling, that had almost become fixed, had acquired a hint of the unknown.

And now there was Emma! Her body, her sex, her bold openness and insistence, all filled him with indescribable repulsion and fear. He felt as if this was the cold snake that had once scared him. In Emma's behaviour there was no gentleness, no trust, no warmth or safety. With her it was all horror. But a horror that drew him in.

They were walking across the mown field on the hill. Sharp moonlight poured across the earth. They could see their shadows in front of them. His was angular and long, it moved its legs in time with his, and he felt as if he had short legs and an enormous body. He looked up at Emma, walking in front of him. Her shadow fell to the left, it was less distinct, it broke as the ground rose and fell to the left of the grassy path on which they walked. When the path widened into a grass strip where the plough had turned, the shadows disappeared. The grass was darker than the light grey stubble, and the shadows sank into it.

He looked past Emma into the valley. It was carved out like a trough, stretching into the distance towards the south, rising on the other side to dark heights. The moon was so clear that he could see the road winding along the valley. Around it gathered clusters of roofs, which formed the villages. For a moment he thought the road was a long snake-like animal with dark swellings along its body, the tail becoming lost in the plain and the head embedded in the hills that closed the valley. The thought of the snake surprised him unpleasantly as soon as it appeared and he wanted to repel it. As he looked at the dark swellings along its body, those villages, it struck him that they could be legs, protruding to right and left, and that the road might be more reminiscent of a lizard than a snake. But then the thought of a lizard was as unpleasant to him as that of a snake.

Emma was walking in front of him; she did not look back once. Because the grass was wet with dew and they had been walking on it for some time, his bare feet were starting to feel cold. His soles did not feel the sharp stubble since he always went around barefoot and they had hardened, but the coldness of the dew ate into his skin. After a while, though, the tingling became burning and it felt as if dew was hot. When he thought about this for a while, he decided that what he was feeling was the warmth of the blood in his veins. The slope was ever steeper and in some places the fields were carved into the hillside like terraces. Here the grass strip narrowed to steep steps. To left and right grew alders and acacias. Emma disappeared into the dark trees. Slowly and cautiously, so as not to slip, he entered a hollow. Beneath his feet the hill began to level out as it ran towards the village and the road.

Emma gestured to him and put her finger to her lips. He leaned his left hand against the trunk of a large tree. They stared at the cluster of houses about a hundred and fifty metres away. The barking of dogs could be heard briefly. They were not barking fiercely, but negligently, out of habit. Then there was silence. In some houses lights could be seen, others were in darkness, as they had windows on the side away from them. Emma looked around as if weighing up the evening quiet that lay over the settlement. Lower down to the right, beside the road, stood a house on its own, illuminated more than the rest. There was also a light in the yard, so that the entrance door could be clearly seen. That door opened a number of times, a person emerged, moved around at the back of the house and then returned across the yard. The sound of a door slamming reached the alders. Then there was silence. No one was moving around. In the upper part of the village the dogs barked again, but soon stopped.

As they went across the field towards the solitary house, Janek thought that the dogs might have been disturbed by the moon. That's what farmers always said, and that night the moon was much brighter than usual. He looked at it. It wasn't full, there was a deep bite out of the right side. Around the illuminated part floated a pinkish halo that also slightly covered the moon's surface. The sky was completely clear; to the south, over the plain, there was a bluish haze and to the north patchy clouds that were not moving anywhere. The night was so unusually light that it disturbed him. It was as if the light originated from an invisible sun, not from the hazy crescent moon. The bluish haze to the south also bothered him, it kept arousing confused associations that he was violently trying to resist. His thoughts returned to the dogs that barked unnecessarily at night and he began to think about this canine habit in order to halt the flow of unpleasant images. He had the feeling that any kind of memory could transform him in a moment and the whole sense of purpose inside him would collapse, since that evening everything was decided inside him. He was calm, he knew exactly what was going to happen and he had resigned himself to this without knowing why he wanted to take part. In reality, this wasn't his conscious will, it was something else altogether. He felt an unusual humility before this young woman, before Emma, he bent himself to her will, he was convinced that he had no choice. He didn't know that this was just an excuse for his inability to resist and free himself from her.

They crossed the stubble to get to the isolated house at the lower end of the village, then came upon an orchard that lay above the house and rose up the slope. A grass strip ran down the hill. Beside it on the slope were the dark outlines of three poplars. The grass strip ran straight towards the illuminated yard, and was separated from the orchard by a low hedge. Emma gestured for him to jump over.

Then she whispered to him what he needed to do. He had to wait for her by the alders, where they had stood before, where the ground descended in steps, she would be quick. Then she went down the grass, across the yard and knocked on the door.

He moved lower in the thick, long grass, crouched down behind an apple tree and listened. Silence. Emma once again banged on the door. It rattled. Once more all was silent for a moment. Then there was a creaking sound and a man's voice said something. The door slammed, a key turned – silence. Then the light in the yard went out. The darkness slowly dissipated and the moonlight fell where before there had been electric light. The grass in the orchard was very high, it had not been mown yet, the apple trees were very close together, with low branches, some hanging down to the ground.

He crossed the wet grass, which soaked his trousers to the knees, and approached the rear of the house, then crouched down behind a dung heap. The back part of the house had a thatched roof that was disproportionately high compared to the walls, as if a small child had pulled a grown-up's hat onto its head. This place was surely the stables that Emma had referred to. A motorbike roared along the road, and he saw the beam of light go past behind the house. The noise receded to the north. Silence again. A long silence. His legs hurt from crouching. He looked up the hill, at the poplars, then again across the dung heap, towards the door.

Then there was a rattling noise, a key turned, the door creaked open, a beam of light fell across the yard as far as the dung heap. Janek flattened himself against the ground. Someone laughed in the house. A wooden cover creaked, footsteps went down to the cellar. Silence. The footsteps returned, the wooden cover fell, the light vanished, a key turned – again silence. That's what Emma had said: someone will go to the cellar for wine, then there'll be no one, and then…

The orchard widened to the right, there were cherry and plum trees packed close together, before the road there was a high hedge that had not been trimmed, following the wall of the house. He quietly moved past the back of the stable. At the end of the wall, where the rear part of the house joined the front, there was a window. A light shone through it. The grass here was cut. He wouldn't need to go so far, just up to… but then he threw himself to the ground. A dog was barking in the yard. It must have been a big one, since its bark was deep and hoarse. When it had barked twice it let out a growl, then it sounded like a chain was being dragged along the ground; evidently it was chained up, just as Emma had said.

When the dog fell silent, Janek did not move for some time. He raised his eyes and felt for the part of the roof that reached beyond the wall of the house. Yes, there were two beams there and an opening in between through which hay could be thrown into the hayloft in the summer. Beneath this opening a wooden door had been built into the wall, closing the entrance to the barn. This door had strong horizontal laths. He silently climbed up and rolled through the opening into the hayloft, which had a strong aroma of hay. On the right, Emma had said; there was a way through the wooden barrier, then a chimney and next to it a hatch. He crawled across, the hay quietly rustling. Soon he felt the wooden barrier and a wooden handle, the hinges creaked and he stopped breathing. He slowly pushed, but it creaked, so he froze.

He held his breath. Nothing happened. He crawled to the other side. He felt around in the dark and touched the brick chimney. He embraced its rectangular mass. Then he leaned over and felt on the floor. Only dust. He turned more to the left. Finally his fingers made contact with a wooden hatch and a chain for raising it. He took a few deep breaths. It struck him that it would be worse for him the more he lingered. When his blood stopped pulsing in his head he took hold of the chain and slightly raised the hatch. There was a ladder beneath, leading to a lit hallway. Nothing. He raised the hatch further and leaned it against the chimney. He put his foot on the first rung. Silence. Then the next rung. A cat meowed in the attic. The noise struck him in the chest like a knife. He began to feel afraid. The cat fell quiet. Onwards. His heart was pounding. Forwards. He was in the hallway. The door to a room.

Now he felt terror. He could no longer control it. His head was buzzing. He was inside the room, he felt for the switch and turned on the light, he looked around and there was the cupboard. The bottom drawer. He pulled from his pocket the key Emma had given him. He inserted it and turned it, the drawer creaked, he snatched the package from the right corner, closed the drawer, locked it, rushed to turn off the light, then he was on the ladder and in the hayloft, he grabbed the chain, it slipped and the hatch fell! A loud crash echoed through the house.

He felt a chill run down his spine and threw himself down blindly. He found himself in the hay. Below someone was talking loudly, the hatch was raised and a torch shone at the other side of the loft, where there was all sorts of junk. Some planks of wood were leaning against the roof.

'What is it?' someone asked from below.

'The cat knocked over a plank!' came a deep voice from the loft. The light flashed and the hatch fell. The voices below fell silent.

For quite some time Janek crouched in the hay. There was a kind of mental and emotional chaos within him. Only after a while did he realise that he needed to get away. He scuttled across the hay like a rat, through the opening and down the ladder. A light was shining through the window among the plum trees. He felt inclined to see what was going on inside, and hurried over to the window, standing on tiptoe to see inside. In front of the window was a table with a bottle, some spilled wine, glasses. Further away, against the wall, was a bed. On it lay Emma, pulling her skirt up over her thighs. A tall, thin man was standing in the middle of the room, fastening his trousers, another stood by the door. These were the Klemars. Janek had never seen them from close up. The thought flashed through his mind that they were extremely ugly. Once more he fixed his eyes on Emma, who rolled to the edge of the bed and put her bare feet on the floor. Her hair was tousled. Then he hurled himself away from the window, across the orchard, across the stubble. A dog barked after him. He rushed up the hill.

He fell into the darkness among the acacias. From the valley came a tumult of voices. Before his eyes large round lights flashed on and off, they kept bursting and flying through the air. Then there were lines of falling snow. Strange images were woven inside him. He uprooted a large tree and kicked it into the air, ran across the river and water beneath his feet felt hard. Then he was buried in gravel. The leaden noise ceased, darkness came, the silence resounded slightly in a metallic kind of way. It was steady and seemed to last forever. And then it burst. Emma was crouching beside him.

'Did you bring it? Did you bring it?' she asked, grabbing hold of him. She snatched the parcel of money from him and stuffed it inside her blouse. She was breathing deeply, exhausted. Suddenly she threw herself back and opened her arms wide. 'Now you can,' she said, gasping for breath. 'Janek!'

He didn't move.

'Are you going to, or not?' she hissed impatiently, raising herself up slightly. Then she lowered herself again. 'The ground is cold. I'm cold. Be quick!'

She pulled up her skirt and spread her legs. 'Can't you see I'm waiting? Stick it in! Can't you do it, or what?'

She sat and stared at him strangely. Tears were running down his face as he looked at the valley. He was trembling.

'You said you'd like to. I'm here, you can have me. In the future, too. Whenever you want. What are you howling for, you're not a kid any more…'

Her voice had become a whisper. A strange fear was emanating from him. As if she felt he was ashamed, afraid. She wanted to help him, and reached for him briskly in order to undress him…

'Leave me alone! Leave me alone!'

The yell that was torn from him expressed such anger; it was so hoarse and loud, that it turned her aside.

'I don't want to!' he yelled again.

She hadn't often heard him speak and did not know his voice, but in that moment it seemed to her horrendous. She didn't understand what it meant, what was wrong, what she had done, what she should have done. She sat there dumbly, shaking.

'Everyone else would like to and I won't let them, but you… you don't want to? But I'd like to do it with you, I really would…'

He emitted a throaty, discordant laugh, the laugh of a grown man. Emma unthinkingly turned round to see if anyone else was nearby, for it seemed to her impossible that such a child could laugh in that way. But she saw he was trembling as if the laugh was shaking him deep inside.

Then he leaped to his feet and ran up the hill.

She rushed after him. Higher up, on the grass strip, he fell. He pounded the earth with his fists. She threw herself upon him.

'Janek, take me, I said! Otherwise I'll be angry, I'll cry. Do you hear me?'

'Leave me alone!' he screamed. 'You already did it with them. Isn't that enough?'

'You saw?' She crouched down and was quiet for a moment.

Then she threw herself on him once more.

'Janek, I had to. What are you thinking of? You knew it would be like that. How else could you have taken the money? You're strange…'

Her voice quivered. Then she whimpered and whispered in his ear:

'Janek, my little Janek! Don't be offended. I'll be yours, I won't go with them anymore if you're angry. Do you hear, Janek, I'd like to do it with you. I'd like to!'

'Go away,' he howled. 'I don't care about them! I don't care!'

'I don't want to,' he said more quietly, after a short pause. 'I don't want to.' Then his eyes scoured her face. 'Why do you do it? Do you enjoy it?'

She looked at him, startled. 'Don't you?'

'No!' They stared at each other. 'I'm scared.'

'What of?'

'I'm afraid.'

'I don't understand.'

Silence.

And then he sprang up and hit her. Her face, her breasts. He fell on her, biting and kicking and throwing punches.

'Janek!' she cried out.

She freed herself, rolled away and got up. 'Why are you beating me?'

He looked at her in horror. 'Don't you like it?'

'You fool!' She darted up the hill as if she had seen a ghost.

She was already far off when he heard her panting and muttering frightened words. She fell and got up again. Then she vanished.

They came three days later. Emma was taken away. The next day they came for him. He met Emma again in a room with a long table, behind which sat a fat, red-faced man in a blue uniform. Two more of them stood by the door. He'd often seen such people before. But now they had come for him, directly for him. It was hot in the room, and flies were buzzing here and there. It also smelled of varnish, as if the door had just acquired a new layer. The Klemars entered.

'Lad!' said the fat man at the table. He had a dumb look about him that radiated laziness. He was breathing heavily.

'Lad!' he repeated. 'Do you know the farmer Klemar and his brother, here present?'

Janek nodded.

'Do you know Emma Baranja, gypsy, here present?'

He nodded again.

'Listen!' The chubby man raised his voice slightly. 'If you tell us the truth, you can go home immediately and nothing will happen to you. Understand?'

Janek nodded.

'Emma Baranja,' the man continued, 'gypsy, here present, is suspected of stealing money from the farmer Klemar. She is accused by Klemar and his brother. When questioned, Emma Baranja denied stealing the money.' Here he fell silent for a moment and stared for some time at the papers in front of him. 'She said it was like this… You stopped her in the woods when she was returning from the village and you persuaded her to… with you… you know very well what I mean… and you offered her money, quite a lot of money. She asked where you got it from and you said you stole it from Klemar. She grabbed the money from your hand intending to run off, but you attacked her and wanted to… by force… and she barely managed to escape. She wanted to return the money to Klemar. Now lad, you tell us if all this is true. Otherwise you'll receive a good hiding, you understand?'

The man struck his fist so hard on the table that the whole room shook. Janek felt a chill.

'Come on lad! Did it all happen as Emma Baranja claims?'

Janek nodded mechanically.

The fat man's face beamed with satisfaction and victory. He puffed himself up, as if he had won a great victory.

'How old are you, lad?' he said with a gentle voice.

'Fifteen,' said Janek, hollowly.

'Fifteen,' repeated the man. 'I can't lock you up because you're too young. We'll have to punish your mother, we heard that you don't have a father. We wanted to send you to an institute for young offenders, but it sounds as if you are good at school – probably a mistake if you ask me, but that's what the teachers say. And the priest spoke up for you, although we don't place any great weight on what the priest says… and some farmer up there, name of Geder, stood bail for you. He says he'll send you to the town so you can study. That's of course nothing to do with us… Geder will answer for any offence you commit. You understand, lad?'

Someone touched his arm. He turned.

No one.

PART TWO

Seven years later, in Ljubljana, he was walking towards the castle that seemed to float in the air like a silhouette, but he wasn't entirely convinced that he was walking along the road. He could feel firm ground beneath his feet, while alongside him ran hazy lines that might have been the edges of the road, yet his sense of the hardness beneath his feet came and went. One moment it was stronger, the next it faded, and at times it disappeared altogether. Then he felt nothing. There was a mist before his eyes, in his ears. His thoughts were sinking as into a deep swamp: not a muddy one; more like quicksand. The only thing he could register was the fluctuating rise and fall of the temperature of his blood. It swung from incredible heat to intense cold, and was different in different parts of his body at the same time. As if he had his right hand in boiling water, his left hand in ice. And so he could neither evaluate the strength of his feelings nor identify their exact location.

He had no sense of time and could not determine how long this absence lasted, this sinking into his own blood. When the temperature fluctuations stabilised, he first of all felt his hearing becoming clearer. He could hear a church choir in the distance, accompanied by an organ, it sounded hollow, as if echoing off the walls of a deep well. The music flowed over him like the waves of hot and cold had before, then it began to settle and intensify, to float. And then the organ keys came to the fore, louder and sharper and crisper. Finally it was all repeated in an even tone. Then there was a sound like human steps. As the sound came nearer, it seemed to him again that he was walking along the road and the hollow steps he could hear were his own.

Almost at the same time, his sight began to clear. The mist condensed into patches and withdrew: to the left and right there were sometimes pulses of flashing light. He thought perhaps they were puddles and that sunlight was reflecting off their surface. But the mist did not lift completely, so he saw nothing with any clarity. The world intruded on him, but not as sharply as to awaken his tired, sunken thoughts. He had a slight feeling that things were moving in a particular direction, that they were going only forwards and not backwards or in many different directions at once. Objects swam around him like balloons, floating above and behind him, circling, approaching and retreating, sometimes seeming to swarm together. The whole time his perceptions remained coarse, hazy. Nothing around him changed, but rather moved at a certain distance, and if they did come nearer they did so only as outlines, never clearly visible. He perceived the reality around him, but found no connection between the outlines and himself. It was as if he was excluded from the real world; as if he could not touch things; as if he was floating on his own, to an extent determined by the flow of his blood, and that things were also floating independently, without contact with him, remaining outside him.

At such moments, more frequent in recent years, a wild restlessness always gripped him, the urge to leap and bang and hurl things around and smash them. He was aware of these feelings, but he never worked out at what level of withdrawal they occurred. Nor could he ever push them away, they had to disappear on their own. They were like pain, and his will was irrelevant. Whenever they appeared, his heartbeat increased, something reminiscent of extreme joy arose in his chest, a yell, but he was also full of other, very different feelings – hatred of his surroundings, wantonness, a craving for violence – he himself called it a craving for violence and nothing more, because he always had to take hold of something and break it, he had to rush around the room and shout and bang his feet on the floor, and only then could he calm down. But at times the attack would be so strong that he was left trembling when it passed. Sometimes he looked with relish at the windowpane and thought how it would be to smash his fist through it and reduce it to fragments – what a sense of relief he would feel! Mostly the mere thought of the act was enough.

He thought that perhaps the attic room where he was staying was at fault: There wasn't a day when he didn't look out the window and see rain. His view was hemmed in by blackened, lichen-covered roofs, which spread into the hillside at strange angles. This was the old part of town and buildings clung to the slope like rotten grapes. If he wanted to see the sky he had to lean far out of the window. But he never did so, he got used to there being no sky in this part of town. As the roofs clustered in front of the glass pane, dusk came early and if it was raining, it was already hard to make out objects at four in the afternoon. There was also a constant noise from the gutter. The rain quietly pattered; not heavy, not a downpour, but more like a grey curtain, every day. Its falling cast a strange silence, which crept through the window, climbed the dark walls, across the low hanging ceiling. The silence irritated him. With the silence came a sense of remoteness, bodily spasms, the urge to destroy.

In one such mood he saw a cat climbing up an almost vertical roof, trying to claw its way to the top. But the roof was slippery, the cat slipped and rolled towards the edge; it tried to grab hold of the gutter, but was unable to and tumbled into the deep yard below, where it lay almost immobilised. When Janek saw this he felt a strange delight, which scared him since he was unable to explain it. But it brought relief: as if he'd been choking and then suddenly breathed air.

After everything remained unchanged for some time, his hearing became sharper again. The first time he noticed it was with the sound of his footsteps. Whereas before they had sounded as if at a distance, now they were right beneath him, very close, and they rattled through his legs towards his stomach. At first, this rattling did not cause him any pain. At every step the shock slid to his stomach, but it took the form of a sound rather than pain. For some time he was suffused with the sound of footsteps.

He suddenly had the feeling that the shocks were caused by the earth. As if the street was pressing hard on his soles, like a fist from below. He was slipping from his floating state and becoming ever heavier. The blows from the earth took the form of pain and he felt very clearly that in spite of the unpleasant feeling his weight was not being pulled down, into the earth, but that the earth was pressing against him. The blows became increasingly intense until he felt as if the ground was beating his feet. Because his thoughts were still mired in quicksand, he did not know how to put all this into words. The ground was neither warm nor cold, there were no specific feelings, nothing that could be defined. It neither burned, nor stung, nor hurt, nor pricked; everything was concentrated in the fact that he could feel the ground, and the feeling was intensifying. Instinctively, he lifted his feet high, wanting to keep them in the air as long as possible, then he began to jump, his feet twitching as if they were bouncing off the ground. The ground was becoming flexible, but his legs were going numb. It felt as if he wasn't moving at all, rather that the ground beneath him was wrinkling, folding and giving way, forming waves and washing him forward like water washes a small leaf. A vague awareness that he was running arose. His hearing failed again, the focus of his awareness shifted to his legs, which were numb, right up to his hips, as if they were not part of him. His sight was still functioning to some extent and with its help the spark of realisation that he was running, for the balloon-like objects around him were whizzing past more rapidly. They were crammed together in greater density, merging together and swimming from one field of vision to another. Only when he began to be assailed through the swarm of balloon-like objects by a sharper light – ever sharper – did he clearly feel he was lifting and putting down his feet in rapid succession. The light was stopping him, his hearing was triggered and he suddenly heard again that he was gasping for breath: his chest was heaving, and he felt his hair clinging to his sweaty forehead. The ground slid beneath him, rotated and stopped. Again it seemed to him that it was his legs that were moving, or rather had been moving, for the next moment they stopped again.

Whenever Daria was with him things unfolded in a similar way. Lust quickly peaked, his tendons flexed, he was gripped by a desire to throw himself at her and strike or bite or pull her hair if she was lying on the couch thinking, or perhaps dozing. Beneath the cover she was naked, for she never dressed until she had decided to leave. The thought of her nakedness always held him back, stopped him throwing himself on her, caused him to listen. Usually she was breathing very lightly. At such moments he would not touch her skin. His lust began to wane as soon as he occupied himself with the question of why her skin still excited him. Before falling asleep they always talked. She asked questions and he answered. Sometimes she seemed pushy, because she kept raking over his past, petulantly, as if it was of immense importance to her to know what had happened to him at different times. But lust always appeared when she was already asleep, when the room was at peace, which was intensified by the pattering of rain. Only then did he sink into the darkness from which he had previously been expelled.

Before him was a road, now he could see it clearly. He realised he was soaked in sweat, rivulets ran from his forehead, he was tousled, he was breathing deeply, he was agitated, he had awoken from his strange state. He felt he was in the darkness, that he had come from the darkness, which he could not understand. He wanted to look back, for the darkness he had come from was evidently behind him, but he was suddenly gripped by fear, constricting his throat. He wanted to get rid of it at all costs, push it back inside him, he felt his face to reassure himself with his own proximity, his eyes leaped around, attaching themselves to objects as if he was drowning and was feeling for roots in a river. On his right there arose from the haziness the sharp outlines of stone houses, in his ears the wind rustled and a slight chill licked his neck. In front of him there really was a road strewn with stones, but the silhouette of the castle was far off, barely visible. A rainy smell flooded his nostrils, a smell of dampness, of depths, of decay. All that seemed to him far away, out of reach, now slowly fell into the dark depths inside him. His thoughts escaped from the quicksand, they seethed in his brain, clear, measurable. He walked across the wide square towards the tavern at the other end of town.

Walking up the wide steps, he entered through the open door. In doing so he felt he was being followed, that someone was mounting the stairs right behind him, and he could feel their breath on the back of his neck. After three steps he went higher and then straight ahead, past the beer hall on the right and the café on the left. The oppressive shadow of the stalker slipped away. When he finally half turned, he saw a shaky old man with a walking stick struggling through the heavy entrance doors. A heaviness grew within him that he wanted to dissipate with a burst of laughter, or a reckless cry of joy, but the feeling passed when he awkwardly swallowed his saliva. He opened the double glass doors in front of him and went inside; one of them closed too quickly and struck his back. He went straight towards the toilets, down two flights of stairs to the cellar. The urinals were yellowish, he saw them clearly, they shone before him as if suspended in the air. It was as if he saw them and nothing else.

Hastily, he unfastened his trousers to urinate, for he felt an enormous pressure in his bladder. His body was already expecting the kind of relief that floods the veins when a tormenting tension is disposed of. His expectation was so strong that it came like a blow to him when he simply stood and stood, and not a drop emerged. The pressure began to subside, it seemed that relief was already on its way, but then unexpectedly the pressure increased again, this time in his stomach, then it leaped to his back, slid up to his throat and into his mouth. It forced him to cough, but it was very dry, nothing like a real cough – as if his mouth had opened of its own accord. As if the pressure in his body had escaped through his mouth.

It helped him a lot to talk to her, to confess. She was no ordinary woman, she kept trying to define him, she had an opinion on his every step, some of his actions she foresaw before he had even formed them in his mind. He always thought this was because she felt something for him. After his secondary school years, when the idea was planted in his brain that his behaviour was unpleasant, deceitful, revengeful, reckless and that there was something fundamentally wrong with him – years when he had got used to being looked at with disapproval, with a raised finger, with disappointment – this woman was special, different, something beyond his imagination.

'You're not a normal person,' she often told him. 'You don't belong in the crowd – not because you have different characteristics from ordinary people, but because in you these characteristics are in different proportions, which are constantly changing. I haven't managed to work out why they change, because in regard to these changes you are powerless, a tragic figure, and in certain moments not responsible for your actions. That in itself is not tragic, but you are responsible to others, you are responsible to the mass of people who have their opinions. They are not interested in causes and circumstances, but only events, results. You were created by events. Nothing is as important for someone's state of mind as what he experienced in childhood. At that time you only perceive, you only realise, but you can't define anything, you don't have enough reasoning power to get to the bottom of things. If at that time things are placed in the wrong slots and those things are so strong that they cut into your soul, then they shape your mind, which with the years gets strengthened and added to, so that reason can no longer change it. Reason comes too late. The organism reacts as it is accustomed to doing. If I knew your past in detail I could tell you why you are not responsible for some of your actions. You're ruled by your instincts, you live in the past, where your reason cannot reach. Your reason is limited, but the past you carry inside you is very strong. You are not aware that you react now as you reacted in the past.'

Apart from a slight prickling in his throat, he no longer felt any unease. Then the prickling stopped and in a moment his head rang with what sounded like a metal spoon being struck against the edge of a saucer. Before his eyes flashed a hazy picture: a hairy hand with long bony fingers. The fingernails were bitten, black and decaying, and a little above the wrist the arm disappeared into the sleeve of a filthy check shirt. Geder's shirt. Between his fingers was a metal spoon. It rose and fell evenly, striking the edge of a yellowish saucer. Then the image in his eye glinted and right in front of him he saw the smooth surface of a smooth wall with drops of water running down it.

He went over to the washbasin, turned on the tap and splashed water in his face. Then he watched the water run down the plughole. As it ran away, the metallic sound in his head faded. When the last of the water gurgled in the pipe and with a pop was replaced by air, there was a similar pop in his head: as if the saucer against which the spoon had been clinking had disintegrated. Another image danced before him. He saw the fragments of the saucer and the spoon lying on the table. But this only lasted a moment, a blink of an eye and it all disappeared with a pop. Once again, as some moments before, he felt a lump in his throat containing a burst of laughter, the beginnings of a sudden yell, a gasp, like someone who was suffocating but then the air rushes into his lungs. Just like before, the lump disintegrated before it could become a sound.

All at once, he noticed a stench in his nostrils, and the objects around him moved closer. He realised he was standing in a badly lit toilet. A fat fly was buzzing from one corner to the other. Water was dripping from the pipe into the urinal and from there onto the floor, like rainwater from a roof. There was also water on the floor, several centimetres deep. All the outflows were blocked and so the liquid, including stuff from other people's bladders, was collecting there. The window just below the ceiling was hermetically sealed and there was a dense, terrible odour in the air. As soon as the stench entered his nostrils, his feet started to move of their own accord and he headed for the door. First up three steps, then straight on for two metres and then three more steps. He was already at the door. He had started to open it when he realised his trousers were still unfastened. He opened the door completely and went along the corridor, fastening his flies with his right hand.

At that moment, a woman approached from his left, saw what he was doing, she went past, turned to her right and started up the stairs that led to the first floor. She looked at him once more, first at his hand and trousers, then she raised her eyes to his face and in the next moment she had disappeared round the corner. But for a moment they had looked at each other and he thought he saw in her eyes a shamelessly inquisitive look directed at the hand fastening his trousers. The incident weighed upon him like a heavy load. In his chest began to grow a strange sorrow, a kind of burden that disabled him, his feet stopped and he stood in the corridor…

The woman had seen him fastening his trousers… He could trace the thoughts that must have flashed through her mind… evidently his behaviour hung in the air before her… he entered her mind and remembered with her, thinking about himself … how he had approached the urinal, how he had unfastened his flies, how he had reached for his member, how he had pulled it out, held it… she must have pictured his sex organ… perhaps in her hands, perhaps she had imagined sex with him… He felt as if he was being pressed to the ground, in heavy chains, suddenly captured, tied up, his freedom lost – he felt guilty before this woman. Curses and accusations rose inside him: now he hated himself for being so careless, for appearing before her at a moment when he was fastening his flies, thus triggering a landslide that shut him off in an incomprehensible dependence.

As soon as he realised that the woman was touching him with her thoughts, she was there within him. Inside and beside himself he felt her proximity. He felt her as a burden, as a nuisance. He stood there, paralysed, and tried to shatter the clear image of her that still floated before him, to distance her and transform her into an outline. He took a step and, oddly, the woman did the same. Once again she stood before him, looking sharply into his face and then at the buttons on his trousers. Her look radiated curiosity, intrusiveness. Again he made a physical effort to take a step aside, this time backwards, but the woman floated after him, he even felt her breath on his face. He began to wave his arms around to defend himself. While doing so he pushed through the doors into the beer hall, ran into a mass of some kind and turned round in a flash: the picture shattered. In front of him stood another woman, whom he had just stumbled into. He gawped at her with glassy eyes.

'Damn gypsy!' she cursed, moving round him and disappearing. As if in the distance, he heard these two words like an echo. But they whooshed towards him and echoed inside him. They were sharp and sounded like a scream. In front of him was the beer hall, there were some men standing at the bar. Nobody looked his way. He went over and looked at the waitress. 'Damn gypsy!' she too said to him. Her voice was old and repugnant, even though she was young, and her eyes were like a vulture's. 'Damn gypsy!' said a low male voice to his right; he turned and saw a well-dressed man in a hat, looking at him indifferently. 'Damn gypsy!' hissed a voice to the left; he turned and found the voice was that of a young guy with messy hair. 'Damn gypsy!' said the whole row of them. 'Damn gypsy!' rang out from the speakers on the wall. The glass doors swayed and whispered deeply: Damn gypsy. From the walls rebounded a thousand voices: Damn gypsy!...

He leaped back, tension building inside him, his lungs gasping for air. He yelled for them all to shut up. It was a hoarse, uncomprehending cry. His voice did not rebound. There was a tomb-like silence in the beer hall. Everyone turned and stared at him with a scared look, as if he were a ghost. He trembled, feeling the coldness of the cement floor beneath his feet. Again a fly buzzed. Quietly, far off.

Deafness assailed his ears, blindness shrouded his eyes, the cement floor detached itself from his paralysed legs, everything sank, and he floated off. The sense of floating was interrupted by the unexpected peace outside. Before he had gone inside, it had seemed to him that the world was swarming around, beneath and above him; that sometimes it even passed through him like a cold wave – a wave of faces, houses and objects. Now everything was motionless, as if the world had turned to stone. The crossroads were empty; the streets on three sides were empty. Even the cars were not moving, but stood there like scattered stones. People, too. Their appearance was rigid; perhaps they were talking, but no one was waving their arms, no one shaking their head, no one changing their posture. Not even the creases on the women's skirts moved. The stony chill had fixed him to the ground and flowed into his veins. He also stood motionless. His thoughts were clear; they seethed in his brain like bright crystals with sharp edges. Through the stone percolated the sense of a presence, something invisible. He felt that this presence was the cause of his paralysis, yet he couldn't define it precisely because he didn't want to think about it, as if he might fall into even greater dependence.

The only solution lay with her. Ever since they first met the solution was with her. Only with her. They met at a New Year's party: the whole university was celebrating. He wasn't sure what took him there… perhaps the anxiety he felt in the attic room was bothering him enough to send him outside… he wandered the streets for some time, convinced that their abandoned chill would lift the burden from his body. But the anxiety did not go away. He wanted to sit in the middle of the crowd on his own, drink a bit, reflect and watch all the excitement without completely opening his eyes, hoping that it would all float before him… so he went there… and sat there for some time, feeling okay in the swarm of people that did not touch him. Then that fat female professor appeared. As if she'd fallen from the sky she stood before him: 'Come and dance, Hudorovec. Oh come on, of course you know how to dance… if not, I'll teach you…'

His hand flew out and he hit her face, feeling joy as he did so. The woman flushed, she stamped her foot so hard that her bottom quivered, spat in his face and growled 'Stinking gypsy'. Then his hand once more flew through the air and he hit her again, so hard that she staggered. Again, he had a good feeling, but different from before… people were looking now… the woman vanished and he sat there, looking absently into space.

Exactly when she appeared he didn't remember, he just saw a silhouette, felt a movement, cigarette smoke: evidently she had offered him a cigarette.

'I'm sure I deserve a slap, just like the professor,' she said. 'I'm harassing you, like she did. But you're thinking, you're on your own and don't want to be disturbed when you're alone. That's why you came here, I noticed immediately: to be alone among this crowd. I watched you. You were walking beneath the window. I was up here on my own and looked out. Of course, my isolation and yours have nothing in common. I have the feeling that outside you weren't so alone, that someone was bothering you, pestering you. I'd even go so far as to say it was you. You from the past, different, but present. And to find some distance from yourself you came into this crowd, like me… Here everything is moving, floating, you can't feel your body, it flows into this light and moves you… So I understand why you hit her. I'd understand it if you hit me, but please don't. I'm like you, the past hangs on me, too, I can't escape from it.'

She was beautiful: tiny, but beautiful. She smoked nervously, but there was a strange peace in her eyes. When he looked at her he felt satisfied. He didn't know why. He felt he had won some kind of victory, that something nice had happened. He was normally afraid of women, especially if they were beautiful, but this one was different. First of all, it did not surprise him that she was excusing something that others thought unacceptable. She was speaking to him simply and without emphasis, as if they'd known each other for a long time. She wasn't looking at him inquisitively, like other women, she was not fluttering her eyelashes to get his attention, she was not saying she had never seen such a handsome face, that he had fine features – like an Indian prince if he'd worn a turban – she didn't allude to him being a gypsy, that he must be temperamental. She did nothing that other female students had done when they met. She was speaking about something else altogether and with no trace of a hidden agenda. She had made no mention at all of how he looked, as if she could not see his exterior, only what was inside and if she did mention some aspect of his appearance, it was in connection with some characteristic she ascribed to him.

'Your face is unusual, striking. I'm sure you must have been ugly when you were younger, for somewhere behind your current expression lie those features and they even sometimes leap to the foreground. Some kind of suffering gave you a disguise. That disguise is good looks, people say, but there is hatred lurking beneath, violent hatred. That's the impression I get. Your face is more frightening than handsome. It fills me with horror. Because it is cruel. Maybe that's why women chase you. Have you thought of that? Do you feel hatred inside?'

She was without the slightest trace of pushiness or falseness, she emitted an air only of simple obviousness, she emitted a pleasant coolness, an assuredness, determinability. He was drawn to her most of all because she explained his actions and his anxiety, she apologised for him to himself. She seemed the embodiment of perfection, the ultimate law of all things, the namer of all events and feelings. In the end he ran to her and needed her, he clung to her like a root to a riverbank. He entrusted her with what tormented him, his doubts and disharmony, and they confided in each other increasingly.

'Origin and blood are not all that important,' she convinced him. 'A person is created by situations in which one has to react in a particular way. We are created by perceptions of moments. Since these situations are different for each one of us, we each have our own mentality. And the way we think is nothing more than a picture of the past. Grown-ups react in the way that the past has taught them to react. Inheritance plays a part only in the intensity of perceptions and reactions. So we could say that your forebears really are the reason for your excessive impulsiveness, but only if it can be proven that the instinctive side of the gypsy character really is so impetuous. Someone with less intense feelings who experienced what you did would be led in a different direction.'

Imperceptibly, she saved him from solitude and ensured that in company he no longer felt so bad with her alongside him. They went to the theatre, concerts and libraries, then she graduated in psychology and got a job, and invited him to a celebration. 'I see only one possibility for you to throw off the burden of the past,' she said to him. 'Because your reason has borders that do not extend as far as the important events of your childhood, you need to extend those borders. Only reason can help you. Only through reason can you extract yourself from the emotional confusion. Give up studying law – who the hell yoked you to that! You must have listened to the wrong advice. You won't save yourself there… Law is pathetic dogma that deadens the mind rather than developing it. Leave the law and transfer to psychology. Here you'll learn to think, conclude, recognise and demonstrate your feelings. Above all, you have to understand people, in other words yourself, only then can you reach for the scalpel of reason and cut out the thing inside you that drives you to despair and even perhaps to death. Don't worry about your scholarship: if you lose it, I have a job and can help you – I can loan you the money and you will pay it back when you can. When you are used to defining and displaying your feelings, you will know how to dispose of the unpleasant ones.'

He saw no deception or bad intentions in her proposal, but in spite of that he did not take her up on it right away. When they weighed things up, they realised that he would lose the two years of law study and it would be better if he stayed and just attended lectures in psychology.

Then one evening she came again. 'I've been thinking,' she said. 'I've been thinking and it strikes me that reason alone will not help you. It will push you even deeper. Although now it seems to offer a complete solution, I doubt that your mental make-up will allow you cold, clear thoughts that do not need an emotional basis to be reliable. There's also the question of whether it is possible to fight with cold reason against mental deformity and whether reason can help in the confusion arising from the wrong perceptions of the past. Recently I've been experiencing a lot of doubt. It's only now that I see that study has given me nothing but a heap of facts that I am misapplying. Maybe I'm wrong in everything I think about you. Even science can grab the wrong end of the stick and then all your findings prove false, even though logical. I think there should be a special psychology for each person, and that general theories and concepts of the human mind be used only as a signpost to self-deception. All of this increasingly convinces me that the most significant situations in which a person strays are during childhood. Situations that teach a person how to react. So in every case it is necessary to check a person's past and identify the blade that scarred them – and then do something with that blade. Of course, you can't get rid of the causes, for a cause is a cause only when it has an effect and what is in the past often can't be erased. In fact, can anything ever be erased? You need to break the chain of a person's reactions and get him to act differently. But how? Perhaps by letting them reconstruct the event. Then there is the possibility that he will see something that he didn't see before and react differently. I'm thinking about you. Your problem is women. Sexuality. The vagina. There's only one way. Your strange behaviour, your loathing arises from a fear of sexuality. Why, I don't know. So I suggest we try. We make love. Perhaps with me you'll find that your fear, which you first experienced with your mother, is unjustified.'

He couldn't decide. She tried to convince him, but ultimately he had to decide for himself, and she didn't want to lure him into anything in a roundabout way. She emphasised that it was only an experiment, to uncover the complex working of his mind. She began by removing her clothes in front of him. 'You have to get used to naked women,' she said. 'A woman is nothing unusual, a person with a certain bodily construction that enables reproduction and the preservation of the species. But the bodily conjoining of man and woman is not only about reproduction, it is connected with pleasures that are the result of satisfying an urge. In other words, it is about the free play of two members of the opposite sex who find satisfaction in their game. Animals have similar urges.'

That's what she said to him.

'Normally, close blood relatives do not come together physically because children produced in that way are often physically and mentally abnormal. In other words, nature has set boundaries for people, but of course that had no connection with anything, just as your relationship with your mother had not. It's about seeing things through the eyes of a normal person. About getting rid of the fear of this action and learning to enjoy.'

She spent whole afternoons at his place. As soon as she arrived she stripped naked and went about the room laying in various positions, read and talked to him, and the whole time he was forced to look at her nakedness. This lasted about a week and the agitation passed. He got used to it. In the movement of her body there was something calming, non-intrusive, self-evident. Then she said that he had to get used to his own body and to her seeing it. This was more difficult. But he had to take the first step so that the barriers could fall. They spent some afternoons sitting around the room looking at each other's nakedness, while she explained the theory of sexual drive. Finally, she thought the time for intercourse had arrived.

They did this on the couch and it was over quickly. He came after a few moments, withdrew from her, curled up in a corner and started to shake. 'I can't,' he whispered. 'I'd like to so much, but I get so agitated that I feel I'll go crazy. This isn't agitation because of the act itself, this is fear, horror. I think it bothers me that you're not my mother. So far, I've only done it with her. And it was different there. I can't explain it. I think I can only do it with my mother and although then I also feel fear, I feel safe in her arms. I feel she is protecting me.'

She let him cry and he felt easier. 'We won't give up. The problem lies here, and it's here we need to break the vicious circle. Once you have to persist until the end. Then we'd take a step forward. You've got to grit your teeth, you can't give up.'

The next time he tried, he tried to persist in the act, but he felt as if he was falling into a deep chasm; when he came, it brought no relief, he felt even more as if he was choking, he felt dizzy. They agreed that in future he would decide when to continue. Once again, they sat around the room naked.

His legs were completely paralysed. Everything lay around him as in the dead of winter, like a waxwork museum. The upper part of his body was still alive, he could feel the blood flowing, the pulse in his forehead was like small blows, and he felt the will and the strength to move. He wanted to move. He stepped slowly and awkwardly, as if using crutches, feeling that only the upper part of his thighs were working, as if his legs were cut off. He didn't know when his foot left the ground and was lowered again. He walked like a blind man, unsteadily.

On the edge of the pavement, his strength failed him. Dark figures stood there, looking across the square, past the parked cars, over the fence towards the castle that hung in the distance like a silhouette. He couldn't see them clearly, he discerned only their outlines to the left and right, behind him. Nor did he know exactly where they were looking, but he was looking in front of himself, across the parked vehicles and the outline of the castle; it never occurred to him that the others might be looking anywhere else. It seemed obvious that they could see only what he could see. He stood there and tried to lift his arm, to tear himself from his lethargy, for he felt as if he was turning to stone. Then, when he managed to lift his right arm a little, he became scared that he could be frozen in this pose, with his arm raised, like a statue, and he quickly lowered it. The whole time his hearing was inactive, and now his eyelids began to droop, as if he was sinking into sleep. But his mind was still working and dragging him back to wakefulness. He was floating in a tormented state: one moment he wanted to sink into sleep, the next to rouse himself.

The worst thing was that the paralysis did not affect his thoughts, but his senses; his thoughts flew somewhere above him, as if torn from him. He could look upon his lifeless form, floating as if from a distance. He wanted to put an end to this tormented state, his thoughts beat against it, he wanted to tear it, but the process unfolded outside his awareness, within him but not within, outside and yet not outside. Such a state often assailed him before sleep, but not quite like that, only similarly, for in sleep thoughts sank and senses continued to function, whereas here the senses were dead and thoughts alive.

And that time it was the same! When the question came, why Daria was doing this, with what intention, and why he was submitting to her without resistance? She was at his place, it was raining outside, the light on the wall was murky. He moved quickly to the couch, grabbed her by the shoulders, startling her.

'Daria!' he croaked. He stared at the outline of her features through the dusk. 'Why are you doing this? What am I to you? Why do I matter? What's your intention? Why do you want me to have a different attitude to sex?'

She did not reply. She sat up, threw back the cover, reached for her clothes and began to get dressed. 'I'm going,' she said. He watched her movements. When she was ready, she opened the door.

'Tell me!' he almost shouted. 'Tell me!'

For some moments she simply stood in the doorway. He got the impression she wanted to see him clearly through the twilight. And then she said: 'Your problem interests me. I'd like to find out if I'm wrong. I'm a psychologist.'

Then she closed the door. He heard her footsteps on the steep staircase. The rain beneath the window was pattering evenly. He no longer saw even outlines. His head became so clear that the music from the radio somewhere down below screeched through him like an axe blade.

Now he became aware that he was in the square, that there were people around him, but this awareness only increased the terrible sense of physical effort. After a period of time he could not have defined, the sense of floating began to abate. Then something strange happened: at one and the same time he sank into sleep and became conscious. Part of him was lost, distanced, but another part remained present and he could feel it with increasing intensity. And then a moment came when he felt nothing less than every single nerve. It seemed the world was inundating him or that he was growing into the world, for suddenly the world was no longer, there was only him. He could not discern his own dimensions or

82

form, he felt only the pulsating of blood, the hardness of bones, his skeleton, muscles, flesh. He felt substance. He felt that he was that substance – a substance that felt itself as a substance. He remembered this with a flash a little later, when the world once more began to assail his senses, when he came together, when he again narrowed to a central point, whereas before he had extended on all sides and everything that his senses now recognised as his surroundings were filled with bodily substance and nerves.

Once again he stood there, his hand thawing, reaching with it into the air: the icy cold was gone, he was no longer afraid that his hand would go numb. Voices began to resound in his ears. He felt the wind on his neck. His eyes jumped from their sockets, they became light and smooth like oiled ball bearings, they leaped into the surroundings. The people standing close by were distinct, they were talking, some of them loudly. The more they had seemed petrified before, the sharper was their speech now. As if they were shouting at him and because of him. Their voices were varied, they reached his ears with different intonations. Some moments they were short, sharp and distinct, then they swarmed like waves of music, transformed into a confused murmuring that came from far off or almost thundered right beside him, like a collective prayer in church. And then silence fell.

The professor pointed to a chair and rubbed his hands together as if cold. Then he sat behind the desk, picked up the student record book and leafed through it. 'Well, well!' he said with a nod, as if pleased with something. 'Not bad! I've heard this and that about you. You're very independent, impulsive. But from your grades, there's no indication that you're not intelligent…'

'You could be wrong!' Janek interrupted him. The professor looked up and stared at him. The frames of his glasses were so translucent that a blinding light reflected from them. 'Sorry?' he said.

'You could be wrong!' said Janek Hudorovec. 'Grades are not a measure of intelligence. Certainly not with the system of teaching that we have at this university.'

'Just a moment,' said the professor. 'If I understand you correctly, you are denying that the teaching system at this university is adequate?'

'That's correct!' snapped Janek. He felt comforted, as if he had finally found a meaning for everything that filled him with uncertainty.

'An interesting attitude,' said the professor. 'But you certainly wouldn't dare say it if you hadn't already thought it through and had evidence for it.' He removed his glasses and wiped the lenses with a soft cloth. 'Why, for instance, do you doubt that the grades are appropriate? Are you convinced that I won't know how to evaluate your knowledge? That means a vote of no confidence in advance and in your eyes our whole interaction will be fruitless. Are you aware of that?'

'I am, professor,' replied Janek Hudorovec tersely.

'If you're so sure that we are incapable of correctly evaluating your knowledge, why do you even submit to testing? Why come to me at all?'

He put his glasses back on, gave Janek a sharp look and put his hands together on the desk.

'Probably I won't be able to answer. Perhaps my actions made sense up until now – I mean, with the intention of passing the exam. Until I entered this room. Now it seems pointless answering your questions and you confirming whether I satisfy some criterion – pointless, because I have to accept in advance that your questions are appropriate. If I don't accept that, then it's perfectly clear that I don't satisfy the criterion, whatever it is. In other words, we cannot talk, no polemic is possible between us while I have the desire that my knowledge satisfies the objective capacity for some particular job or kind of work! While that desire persists, I have to accept that your questions are appropriate. But it's not clear – and even less proven – whether your questions and the criteria for your evaluation of my knowledge are objectively appropriate. I'm telling you this because it would seem dishonest to keep quiet about my doubts regarding the point of what we are doing in order to achieve a positive grade that would confirm my supposed suitability for some job or work. What I want to say, professor, is that the students know precisely what your criteria are with regard to assessing their knowledge, so their main aim is to satisfy those criteria, not to really learn anything. They want to get past the obstacle – in other words, university – as quickly as possible and with a qualification in their hands throw themselves into the intrigue of collective life. Students see university only as a barrier they have to leap over, for without the right documents the machine will not accept them.'

After a short pause he continued. 'Study at this university is just a struggle for pieces of paper, professor, not for knowledge. And it is easy for anyone who submits to your criteria. It's clear that anyone who is interested only in a paper qualification will take advantage of the absurdity and rigidity of your criteria, and it's here where the big mistake begins. If someone wants to satisfy your criteria he doesn't need to be intelligent, there's absolutely no need for him to know how to think, he just needs to be a little bit cunning and to deceive you with your own words and create the impression that he 'revised' for the exam… Stupid word, revised. Your intellectual training has the failing that a person does not learn to think and draw conclusions – all you do is plant some dogmas in their brain, which very quickly evaporate. And even if they didn't, there is no way they would be able to make any kind of use of them in life. You, for instance, evaluate only whether I have remembered certain rules, dates, quotes, decrees, and you're not interested in my personal attitude to things and how I could defend it. If an hour before an exam a student wants to memorise your rules, he requires no intelligence. So I sincerely doubt that the grades we get are a measure of knowledge or ability. You send into the world premature infants and in doing so you delude yourself that you are an excellent teacher… That's what I wanted to say, professor. Not with the intention of offending you. If I wanted to offend you, I'm sure I'd try a different approach. I merely wish to define my attitude to your criteria and thus give the right shape to our discussion, if any discussion arises during this exam. I am interested in the heart and soul of law, whereas you, it seems to me, are interested only in its formal framework.'

When he stopped talking, the professor stared at his hands on the desk for some time, as if checking that his fingernails were clean. 'Your opinion about my criteria does not offend me in the least,' he said eventually. His voice vibrated slightly, as if he was trying not to exceed its usual volume. 'I know my criteria very well and have been using them for years. But no one has ever challenged them in such a bold way before. I can only conclude that there is some goal you wish to achieve by doing so, but I am unable to work out what it might be. That I send into the world premature infants is nonsense, even you must admit. I don't teach you to think, you must know how to do that before you get here! If you detest the material you have to learn, then I can't help you and I suggest that you go and study elsewhere. And if you have such doubts about my judgement, if you are unable to accept the appropriateness of my questions, as you indicated, since it would be hypocritical, then I don't understand why you came, why you don't give up on exams and why you have this record book. And if the university is a barrier for you, as you claim it is for all the others, then jump over it, it won't be difficult for you, but if you don't need to, then I can't understand what you're doing here. A different university from the one currently available to you does not exist, as you no doubt know! And I have to emphasise that it doesn't matter to me what you do – if you don't want to be examined, then the door is there, I won't be sorry to see you make use of it. If, on the other hand, you want this grade, because you need it for some reason or other, then I am obliged to ask you some questions. It's your decision!'

For some time Janek looked him straight in the eye. The professor did not want to look away first. But staring became unpleasant, so they both suddenly lowered their gaze.

'I feel as if we don't understand each other, professor, and that we won't. You accuse me of having some goal – that is your defence – but I don't… In fact, I do… maybe that's it… it has just become clear to me that I have to stop playing the game, for the rules have become intolerable to me. If I answered your questions now, I'd be doing so tongue-in-cheek. It would be pointless… Maybe it's true what you said; you've no idea what I'm doing here. I don't know either. Maybe I was also looking for a piece of paper, because that's what I was sent here for, that's the idea I've become accustomed to. But because there's nothing I want to acquire through qualifications, because I don't want a bigger slice of the cake, to be precise, there's no point pretending I do. I would be registered by my pieces of paper. But what about the real me, professor? Where would I be? No one would say Hudorovec, but the law graduate, or something like that. In short, professor, I don't want to be documented. If I now had to answer your questions, I would feel as if you were skinning me alive.'

'Mr Hudoróvec…'

'It's not Hudoróvec, professor, but Hudorovec.'

'Of course, my apologies… what I want to say is… wouldn't you still… Look, tomorrow you may see things differently and you may regret what you've said today… You're a very independent young man, a very rebellious young man, and I like that, I must admit… but a slightly more realistic view of the world would serve you better. You'll have to eat, you'll have a family… do you intend to leave university? What will you do, chop firewood, make bricks, sell newspapers? Climb over this barrier and when your future is guaranteed you can concern yourself with such thoughts as much as you like. I can understand that you are burdened by the administrative side of study, because you have more sense of space and independence than is usual… but you need to live, young man, believe me. It won't cost you anything to grit your teeth once or twice a year. Don't let your feelings lead you to make the wrong decision… I'm ready to be as open as possible with you, just say what theme would suit you… But don't do something stupid for which you'd pay a high price.'

'I'd like to thank you for your benevolence, professor. But you're looking at things from a completely different point of view. You're thinking about food on the table and material existence. But believe me when I say that five months without food would not cause me the same torment as would answering your questions now. This is not a rebellion against you, please believe that. I simply can't do this…'

'All right, young man, if it's so repulsive to you to answer questions, give me your record book, I'll give you a grade as if you had answered my questions... I'm sure you're familiar with the material... but don't take any risks... come on... the grade will come in useful when you reconsider.'

'No!' snapped Janek, jumping up from his seat and snatching the record book from the desk. The professor's face showed his disappointment. 'You can't do that, because for me the awareness that I've been evaluated, validated, is worse than being asked questions. I don't want to be documented in any way whatsoever. I shouldn't have come, professor, or I should have left earlier. You're trying to understand me, but you're coming at it from the wrong direction and so in truth you don't understand me at all. We're not going to achieve anything. It's a waste of time. I'm going!'

He stuffed his record book in his coat pocket, turned and went to the door.

It was cold on the street. There was a slight drizzle and he turned up his coat collar. There were puddles on the pavement and water found its way into his shoes. Passing car tyres made a sizzling noise, like hot butter. Engines were revving. On the narrow crossings people were lifting their umbrellas high in the air so they could squeeze past each other... The traffic policemen whistled. The traffic stopped. And then continued...

The train sat at the platform. It had two blue and white carriages that had been washed so clean by the rain that they glistened. It was still drizzling, but in the direction the train was pointing the sky was lighter. Inside the carriage there was a smell of wet coats. It was gloomy. Full. Hats, bald patches, moving heads. Gestures, murmuring. The ticket inspector went past with his clippers in hand. Over there... a woman with children...

'Is this seat free?'

'So far it be,' the woman said with a nod. He was startled by her dialect. It startled him like closeness, and he felt as if he was in another world, a past world. He put his suitcase on the rack, sat down… the soft seat gave way beneath him…

The woman looked at him with curiosity, but not intrusively. Then she stared out the window, only occasionally throwing him a quick glance. Words flew from all directions, long drawn out words with singsong vowels. It was raining lightly but inside it was warm, people were creating warmth. The speech satisfied, calmed… stirred, but also lulled to sleep. He sank into a sense of comfort. Drops ran down the window panes, which were wet and blurred… Outside, on the platform, a large white clock hanging from the roof. A few more minutes… Moments, tiny moments…

People were rushing past with umbrellas, milling around, looking, waiting. An unclear voice came from the loudspeaker, a rainy voice… The carriage shook, below an engine coughed and began to run, they were warming up… A whistle from the left… 'Attention, attention!'… Pouring, crowds, waves of sound… The black hand on the clock jumped a minute. A locomotive with sooty wagons went whistling past… rattling… a flash… The platform again…

He thought he saw Daria in the crowd… that she had pushed her way to the front and was looking in each carriage window… She was wearing a grey coat and glasses… She only wore them at the theatre… She was already at the edge of the platform, she stood there for some time as if thinking something over… She was moving forward, she would come… It had seemed to him that it was over, finished! And now here she was! Dragging things out, trying to reword them… If she wanted to say goodbye, okay, but there was no need.

His first feeling was that she was being intrusive. After all, he was running away, and she was coming after him like a hunting dog… She'd grab him with her teeth and drag him back, onto the rainy streets, to the attic room, she'd tie him up, measure his thoughts… Let's make love… grit your teeth, last to the end… You're not responsible, not responsible… Don't take risks, Mr Hudoróvec, overcome this obstacle, you're not going to be a news-paper seller, surely… Away, away…

S he found him. She's sitting here, beside him. Looking at him. 'Aren't you happy I came?' There's something in her eyes he's never seen before, while in his she sees violent loathing, horror, swollen with revenge. 'I couldn't… I know I can't explain anything to you now. You wouldn't understand, you wouldn't want to understand. You sank out of sight, you're distant, you're living in a different world. I wanted to prevent you returning home, I sensed it would happen. It's my fault, I got it wrong…'

She stopped talking, nervously wringing her hands and looking at her lap. He said nothing. She waited, as if hoping that he would eventually say something. 'If I began to speak of things that you were not used to between us, I would achieve nothing. If I were now to reveal some higher truth, I'd be even more sullied in your eyes. It's clear to me that I can no longer follow you, that you've already gone beyond where my words or those of others can still influence you. Your letter revealed that. You'd been pushed too far. With my efforts to detain you, I probably ensured that you left even sooner. I could say I'm afraid what will become of you, but my fear means nothing. Nevertheless: what will the future bring? Have you thought of that? You're leaving now, okay, but how will it all end? It's been seven years, Janek, everything is different there. Maybe you're returning to a world that no longer exists. And when you discover that, what then? That's what I fear most, for in that moment you will react in the wrong way. I'm sure of that. Have you thought of that? Just tell me that, Janek! Have you thought of that?'

'Listen, Daria, I don't understand your concerns. Besides which, this is totally repulsive to me. You remind me of a wearisome nursery teacher who constantly follows you around, saying what colour's this, what colour's that? Why did you come? I told you in my letter how it was and if you can't understand that, you who always understood me, then… then… I don't know. You come here and start pestering me, although you know all too well how I feel if I am being pestered! You're just a pathetic particle of dust, like all the others. Why are you trying to drag me back? Let me go. Let me return to where I belong. You're different to how you were.

Are you pretending? Either you were acting then or you're acting now. Or you're always acting. Stop being a millstone around my neck. That's all I'm asking you. I don't like you being near me. I don't like it because I can't tolerate it. Why that's so, I don't know and I don't want to think about. It's not your fault, it's mine. Go. Do you understand? Go!'

He was trembling slightly. Her coat smelled of rain. She got up. She offered him her hand. He did not move.

'Won't you give me your hand?'

He stared at her.

'Once I slaughtered some puppies… you know, their insides splattered everywhere…' He grimaced, his eyes darkened. He saw Daria was crying.

A loud, convulsive guffaw burst from his chest, as if a rock had moved – it was violently victorious, a great satisfaction. People turned round. He could barely silence his laughter, and in the end it turned to a kind of loud choking sound, torn from the depths. He saw the girl opposite, wide-eyed, pressing against her mother, leaning over a basket to reach her. The laughter erupted once more, saliva spraying around him as he shook… He saw that people were staring… He became aware he was doing something strange, the guffaw ended. Confused and frightened he stared through the window.

Daria had gone… He wanted to go after her, she must be just outside by now. He pulled down the window, leaned into the rain, the engine coughed, the train moved… She wasn't there… The crowd was swirling… umbrellas… going across the tracks… A voice came from the loudspeaker… The wheels clacked over the rails… He turned to his seat… He sank down… He felt the floor unsteady beneath him… It passed … click-clack, click-clack… Had she not understood him? Maybe the letter he sent her wasn't clear. Yes, it was complicated, contradictory and… the whole time he, too, doubted whether he could express the right things…

Dear Daria

I decided to write to you. You know how hard it is for me to talk, that I don't like talking. This isn't connected with my stammer or with fear, I feel a real need to talk, it brings a kind of relief. But when I hear my voice, it seems to me that I am saying something other than what I want to say: if I shape my mouth to say A, I actually say B. That's why I'm writing. The words are on paper, I don't hear them, so the feeling of their superficiality is less marked. I don't know why I'm so convinced that it is impossible to express what I want. I wondered whether I lacked the words, but I realised I have more than enough. But words themselves do not illustrate thoughts or feelings. A combination of words, the right tone, a word picture is needed if you want to express what you are thinking, if you want to be sure that words do not mock your intention! I can't do that. There are enough words, but they need to be stronger, different. More intense. But they're not. So I get the feeling that you can't say anything with words, at best they're only suitable for referring to visible objects. But we're used to them and in the end they're all we have. So I know in advance that I won't be able to say what I want to say. But even the fact of trying brings me a measure of relief. These words are a monologue, though they are intended for you and you will read them. Through my irregular study of psychology, which I latched onto following your advice, I learned only this: that we are constantly talking only to ourselves, other people are merely a means to this end. Even when I talked to you, you meant only as much to me as I thought I needed to make up my world. Your relation to me is the same. You admitted as much yourself. You said you were interested in my problem. You're interested whether your theory of the influence of events on the human mind is right. You needed me. And you used me. You were frank with me and I'll be the same: when I write to you, I write to myself, I remove the weight of my tormented past, or as you would say I remove it in such a way that you understand it.

I want to speak of my past, although you are convinced that you already know it. That is not the case. Even I only began to think of it some days ago (probably thanks to you, it's true). I want to speak of it, even though I know I won't be able to find my way to the truth. And even if I did succeed, I wouldn't be able to express the truth, for words do not suffice, as I've already said.

So why this letter? Why this desire to talk? I don't know. But the desire is here, I can't resist it (you would say I'm not responsible for some of my actions). Besides which, something tells me I can't leave town without letting you know. In that dark world you were the only one who wanted to do something good for me, regardless of the reasons for your inclination. I have decided to go and you are the only one I want to tell. And the only one who might be interested. Of course, by way of thanks for the good deeds with which you wanted to cure the 'sick' nature of my inner world, as you called it, it would be fitting for me to remain for some time your guinea pig. In that way two things might happen: you would find confirmation of your supposed truth and I would be cured.

I don't believe that's going to happen, so I'm not staying. You yourself said that theories of the human mind are merely signposts to self-deception and in our case, too, that would be the case. Because you approached my mind with a pre-existing model you would quickly uncover in me many things that confirmed your suppositions and anything that did not, you would overlook. Nowhere can you get it wrong so quickly as with the human mind. I'm convinced that it is unknowable. Besides which, the 'sickness' of my inner world would remain. No experiment could cure me. Not even by teaching me about sex. I've already experienced such teaching. That was fatal and I'm sure it is the millstone that I cannot shift.'

The rain stopped. To his right ran a muddy river like a torrent. There was water everywhere. It was getting hot in the carriage, suffocating. People were still blabbering, someone turned on a radio; from it crawled indistinct sounds like worms. The ticket collector came through the door, followed by a cold draught that crept beneath clothes. Then the heat returned, and with it the pressure. The passengers sank into a lethargic absence.

'I spoke about a decision to leave this dark world, but in truth it was not a decision, for a decision is an act of strength. I lost my strength. A decision would only have been possible if I had stayed – leaving is a defeat, as I am well aware! It's my second year here in the capital and the whole time I have felt a longing to return home. Maybe longing is not the right word, more an urge – wild, bloody. This I know only now, when it has been thrown to the surface. These two years have opened up many possibilities, I could have got used to things, but I didn't. I thought it was due to my slow, lukewarm nature, but now I know it's instinctive: I was fighting with the spiders that trapped me in this dark web. For in fact my nature is not slow and lukewarm, but quite the opposite! And all my actions which were condemned as the 'outbursts of an unbalanced gypsy' and which you would say I'm not responsible for, were simply a revolt against being swallowed up by the city.

That fear accompanied me the whole time. Because of it, right from the start I acted in a hostile way to everything around me. That seemed the best defence. When we met, you said that I was tormented by the presence of a person and that this person was my past self. That came like a lighting strike: it seemed so incredible that with your first words you would get straight to the heart of my problem! So I felt no resistance towards you. Hence our acquaintance, which became psychotherapy. From the very beginning, something was driving me back home. And although the 'me' from the past was tormenting the present 'me', it was becoming stronger, tying my hands, dragging me back, as if that 'me', wherever it was, had not settled all its scores. I finally realised that I had to leave, for while that 'me' grew inside, the facts were there. Over two years they became clear, and for two years I suppressed them and fled before them, but now they have caught up with me.

And now I see that there were two processes unfolding inside me. I felt an urge to go back to where I came from, and I resisted this world, so that this place did not completely swallow me up, and at the same time I fought against the realisation that I had to go back, that I had to give in. You would say that my feelings drew me back, while my reason was telling me to stay. But that's not the case. Both processes were exceptionally emotional: I was being pulled back, lured, but the fear of returning pushed me forward. That fear is still inside me, but the urge is stronger. I think that these parallel, contradictory feelings are fundamental and that they appeared when my problem began.

I am afraid of things I don't understand. But at the same time I am strongly drawn to the cause of this fear, because I think it will pass if I uncover the cause. This situation has been repeated in different variations my whole life – flight and return. My reactions always run along this axis and maybe you're right when you say that I'm not responsible for them, since they happen without the presence of reason, completely spontaneously. My resistance to this dark world is the consequence of my desire to go back. Somewhere in the past the causes of my fear are buried and they drag me back. You wanted to solve the problem by 'reconstructing the event'. The question is, whether the sex act really is at the heart of my problem. Whether the possible source of the problem is the circumstances in which things happened. You saw yourself that 'reconstructing the event' did not bring a solution, and I had sensed that before. If the sexual act was supposedly the cause of my fear of sex, then I have to admit that sex between us was very different from that with my mother. I've already told you that with my mother I felt a sense of protection and that feeling was conditional upon her relation to me. My mother always saw me as an unhappy, driven creature whom she had to help, while in her, because of her love and guidance, I found an absolute refuge. When I was gripped by horror upon discovering sex, she wanted to destroy that horror – she wanted to teach me and show me how it was done. When I had intercourse with her, the horror of intercourse was of course present, but in her arms I felt a safety shield and from behind that shield I could get to know that horror, that danger. There was no trace of the pleasure here of which you speak. I know nothing of such pleasure. So from the very beginning, sexuality was conditioned by protection, my mother's protection.

And then our relationship took a new turn… my mother's masochism… I told you about that. With her wish that I physically maltreat her I had to compromise myself for the sake of the relationship, for I loved her endlessly. Thus for me our sexual intercourse was both recognition of horror and the fight against it, as well as gratitude towards her, which expressed itself in concern for her pleasure. I told you that my ideas about sex were very unclear. I didn't realise I was involved in an incestuous relationship, that my mother was a masochist… I loved and respected Geder because I was convinced that he beat my mother to ensure her pleasure. I experienced only the essence of our relationship, I did not know how it looked from the outside.

I have to admit, though, that even later, when I learned the names for these things, the relationship did not change. And today it is no different. This emerges when other women appear. The first was Emma, whom I told you about. You differ from her in that you tried to deal with me through reason. That's why we ended up having sex. That didn't happen with Emma. With you and her there is no feeling of protection, there is no maternal hand, no safety shield behind which to hide and observe the horror. Here, the horror is right in front of me. I find refuge only with my mother. It's her fault that I feel resistance to women. This horror in the face of sex I probably won't be able to describe to you. When I think about it, it all seems so improbable. I understand everything, the theory of sexual intercourse is clear to me and seems simple and mundane – but at the moment the act begins, when I feel I am part of the game, my reason withdraws, my interior world becomes primitive, childish, and fear grabs me by the throat. I can't describe that horror. Perhaps… imagine that you have put a smooth, cold snake on your breast and it is slithering across you… How would you feel?

I often feel the urge to grab hold of something, to beat it, to cause suffering. I fear that my giving in to my mother's masochism has transformed into sadism. I am drawn to her. Our relationship has not ended, it is unresolved – I admit that I am more than ever in its claws! Reason doesn't help me, reason even seems stupid and pathetic, reason seems like the alpha and omega of the world from which I am fleeing. In recent days I feel that I am becoming somehow childish, I don't think as much, but am flooded with sensory impressions. So in reality it is not a decision, it is subservience to inner urges.'

'Although I discovered the reasons for my revolt against the world in which I lived for two years, at moments my 'attitude to the masses' as you would call it, surprises and amazes me. The majority of people my age drive themselves towards the highest possible position amongst the masses, yet I do not strive for that. This might lead some to say that I was abnormal. You know that I have acquired quite a number of 'psychological' labels, which in addition to asociality have hinted at hypochondria, mental retardation and a social complex. If I was part of the masses, then these labels would hurt me, since I would feel that in their eyes I was at the bottom of the ladder. All these young people studying alongside me and making plans for the future want to achieve one thing: success and a name for themselves. They don't realise that in the depersonalised masses of the inferior there are no names, no individuality, no freedom. The name they wish to acquire has no connection with individuality and personal freedom, it is just an emission of the collective, an emission of impersonality. That dark world, that mill of collectively depersonalised young people, blunts their passions, moulds them into puppets that dance like the undulating floor of the collective beneath them. They are not aware that their desire for success in the collective is a signpost to self-deception. Those are the words you would use, for it was you that said I wasn't part of the masses.

I think that way, too, I haven't allowed myself to be swallowed up. But there is no heroism involved, for you know that I was saved from ruin by the past – the very thing that in itself may mean ruin on an even greater scale. Maybe we don't decide at all, but rather possibilities pull us along with them. I don't believe in conscious decisions – behind every human gesture is a background that is expressively instinctive. As soon as someone is brave enough to abandon their illusions, at the end of every possibility there is something bad, something unpleasant. These young people, these students, these pursuers of success are not brave enough.

Because I am an outsider, I am responsible only to myself for my actions. But you saw yourself that it is not so. The masses see me as one of their dust particles and claim that I am responsible to them. But the concept of responsibility is so beyond my capacity to understand it, that I don't even have the courage to discuss it. Yet there is something I can say for certain: the masses change the concept of responsibility in line with their habits, responsibility is directly connected with the tradition – and if we say that someone is not responsible for their actions, we admit that the tradition of the collective has power over them. And that is not the case, as you can see!

When I slapped that professor, when I pulled the truncheon from the police officer's hands and beat him until he bled, when I began to shout in the middle of a theatre performance, when I tipped over the shelves in the bookshop, when I threw the plate under the table in the canteen, and so on and so on – you're familiar with my 'asocial' acts – what did the masses see? A violation of their habits: lack of sense of responsibility, mental retardation, a gypsy complex, an undeveloped personality, hypochondria, vandalism, the beginnings of mental illness… You know the labels. We have to answer to the masses for our actions. I am helpless against their demands. If for no other reason, because I am an outsider. Because I am opposed. The masses are convinced that I'm consciously in opposition to them and it never occurs to them that the reason might lie elsewhere.

Of course, as soon as I joined them and felt remorse for my outbursts, I would get the power to undermine the negative attitude of the masses towards me: I would have adapted to their habits, 'improved' myself. Repentance is evidence that a person does not lack a sense of responsibility. But I have never felt the urge to repent. I only know of it in a theoretical kind of way. I don't apologise for my 'asocial' actions, since they were momentary sensory reactions that cannot be grasped with the reason. For I may yet do something else 'asocial' tomorrow. Why I began shouting during that theatre performance, so that they had to stop it and throw me out, I simply don't know. I sat there quietly for a long time and watched with interest, even though theatre seems ineffably theatrical and unreal – and basically unimportant. I prefer to watch the rain falling. But then I was overcome by restlessness, a desire for action, for something wild. The sense of restlessness was unbelievably great, it built up inside me until I felt I would explode…. And I thought I'd jump on one of the audience… At that moment there was a long silence on stage and that silence only increased the unbearable feeling within me… And then it was as if I'd lost consciousness and animal cries emerged from my mouth… Later they told me that the auditorium froze. The lights immediately came on. People thought someone had been killed. Then I was half dragged, half carried out. The police were called... I couldn't explain myself. Eventually it was 'discovered' that I have a cannibal-like relationship to culture and wished to demonstrate that.

I always said that I didn't know why I did something, but no one believed me. They planted a purpose on me, found causes, branded me as a troublemaker. To the public, I became 'that gypsy who yelled in the theatre, that gypsy who beat up the police officer, that gypsy who has a screw loose...' and so on – you know that my status is tightly defined. You were the only particle of dust in the collective that wanted to see something different in me; the only one for whom I wasn't too miniscule to be a guinea pig in an experiment: Psychology... The boundaries of normality... The Hudorovec case...

But you were open about it. Your experiments didn't bother me, because you aroused a hope in me that my attitude towards the masses was misguided. Besides which, you were a woman and my desire for women is incredibly great, although my fear of them is even greater. With you, my fear was moderated, perhaps because in you I saw primarily intellect. But as soon as I saw you as a woman, the fear struck back. You are without doubt one of the most noble particles, because you have an independent attitude, but you are nevertheless part of the masses and therefore you are the opposition! I've read a number of books about the attraction between men and women – which is also referred to as love – but I see that between us there was nothing like that, neither on your side nor on mine. For you, I was an object of research. That this research was very zealous is shown by the fact that you sacrificed your body, for women do that usually for pleasure.

I, too, feel no real affection for you, although I don't analyse this and I seek no clarification of why it is so. Both of us had fairly distinct wishes and it's completely clear what impulses led to our relationship.'

'I think I'll leave tomorrow evening. I've been thinking about my possible future in this city. And about my future in general: I would no doubt finish my law degree, for it's not really difficult and, as you said, is only dogma. Then my home municipality, which has given me a scholarship, would probably give me a job at the court. You see, my people are already delighted that everything will turn in their favour and have planned how litigious they're going to be. The thing I like most about my race is their naivety. It reminds me of virginity, of something genuine. Something that is far from what you call art and culture. Gypsies have no culture. That's why I think their humanity is less damaged and more effective than the arrogance of this dark society. So, I'd get a job. But I'm not attracted by a job or by the thought of pursuing people through the courts; and because of that study seems barren. That's how far I've dared to think of my future. No further. I considered the possibility that after graduating I would stay in Ljubljana, in the heart of the masses, although outside it, and not return to my province, but that seems even less likely.

It's impossible to logically explain why I would quit studying and give up my scholarship at the very moment when I have a chance of becoming what my people call 'a gentleman', so I won't even try. Evidently, every dust particle is convinced that a normal person will not leave the trough and head for some smelly gypsy settlement where he won't know what to do with himself.

The main reason I am returning is my mother. Our relationship is a prison, so that staying in this town and aimless studying are both intolerable to me. Utterly intolerable. I'll breathe a great sigh of relief when I see this town disappearing through the window. My longing to return to my people has a number of unclear nuances – that wind, the smell of the forest, meadows; the stench of our homes, which may seem unbearable to you, is like a refreshing drink to me…

and the endless plain that I can see from the hill above the settlement – all these things are like a warm bed to which you retreat when it's freezing cold. Talks with Geder, with the priest, and with Pišta Baranja when he was still alive, are the metal fastenings of my mind. Exaggerated homesickness, you would say. But it's not. Because behind it all hides my mother. Homesickness for a vagina? One specific vagina? My attempts to uncover the impulses forcing me home are a barren exercise, I'm aware of that. I don't know why I'm doing it. It's your fault, you taught me to feel my way rationally. Maybe I could tell you more, but my desire to speak has faded away… I don't even know whether I will send you this letter, since it has absolutely no value to you. And at the end of the day, it's more of a monologue.

You will stay here. You won't become part of my past. I'm returning to my past and I hope I'll forget about you completely. You have not left any scars in my mind. You were not a cutting instrument. To use your words… I'm no longer prepared to play the guinea pig, so please let me go. Maybe you'll find evidence for your theory through a theoretical route. Or with someone else.'

PART THREE

Home again! On the edge of the wood the old beech trees were rustling. Their bright young leaves shone in the afternoon sunlight. The sun's rays permeated the thin leaves, so that they were even lighter on the underside, transparent and yellowish. The breath of air that was making them tremble was coming unevenly from the valley. And then, after some moments of stillness, something stirred among the trees, a wind arose, came to the edge, stopped, withdrew unobserved and then reappeared a hundred metres lower. He sat on the roots of an oak tree, listening. The warm waves of air flowed over him and made him feel drowsy. But this was not ordinary drowsiness, for his thoughts were flowing ever more lazily, getting caught up and then lost in the various sounds.

He remembered that in his childhood nature had often flowed into him in just this way. Nature had always worked on him like an opiate. If he sank deeply into it, if he succumbed to its tentacles, it created in him a dangerous imbalance, in which his instincts rose to the surface and bit into his movements. He felt that the material world was defeating him; slowly flowing into him and paralysing him like a narcotic. But in this sinking he sensed a certain sweetness, for he recognised that he was losing his possibility of deciding, losing his willpower, becoming passive, and this removed from him the burden of responsibility.

But now he could rationally define the inflow of nature, which before had not been possible. He could hold it back, if he wanted, and then let it continue a drop at a time, as if taking in a drug. And when he was almost completely groggy, he focused and pushed the air and sounds and objects to a certain distance, from where only their tentacles reached out, tickling him gently. It was a special feeling when those tentacles wrapped round him and drew him in, until nature once more possessed him, before withdrawing once more. That was how he played, letting himself fall into danger. The inflow of the outside world represented a pleasant falling, a sinking that gave him a special pleasure. He felt his body move or his hand rise, and then when the tentacles relaxed their grip a little, his body became ever number. In the end, he could no longer raise his hands, he was overcome by inertia, the outside world concentrated inside him and moved there, he no longer felt that there was a relationship between him and the world, he himself was the world, it flowed in him and with him. But at the same time, he knew that he could break this. Just a little mental effort, various combinations of thought… and the world was already withdrawing, already creeping back, the grip of its tentacles weakening.

Whenever he sank too far, it took him quite some time to return to clarity. There was also a particular pleasure in returning, in the struggle for distinctness when he extracted himself from the writhing tentacles. What was new was that when blending with nature he was aware of it happening. If he wanted, he could withdraw at any moment. That was his strength.

Becoming passive! That was how Daria defined it in her letter – somehow she had found his address. He had been convinced that he wouldn't think of her at all when he finally returned to his own world, but it was not like that. He didn't understand these feelings and drove them away. Then a letter arrived and he was pleased. Perhaps because it arrived precisely at the moment when, for the first time since his return, something fell apart and he got the feeling that there was a wall before him that he had previously not been aware of. After that he began to think of Daria often. Had she not said on the train that everything might have changed, that the old world no longer existed? For quite some time he was not even aware that it had changed, as on the outside it looked the same. Days ran along the same old tracks, people were a little older, but the same as before. Yet there was something in between, a kind of barrier.

'How are you? I know you won't answer me. But by now you've probably realised that time has passed. And time complicates everything, for time includes events. And when you were not there, many things happened that you don't know about. That's what is lacking in your attitude to the world of your past. Every absence is harmful, even though you think you'll benefit from it. If you don't go out in the rain you'll stay dry, but you won't know what rain feels like. Now you have probably looked things in the eye. When you left I was constantly thinking of you. And I came to some new conclusions. I admit I may be wrong, but that's the danger with every conviction. I discovered that your problem with sex is a very broad one – broader than it seems. It has spread to your whole attitude to the world.

The first idea about this arose when I spoke with my sociology professor about your exam. And when I thought about your attacks, it seemed to me that I wasn't wrong. I'm sure that your attitude to the world so far has been completely passive. You are completely without the capacity to decide, without willpower. The whole time you have been surrendering and withdrawing. That, of course, denied the man within. When the break occurred that flung you into passivity, it caused serious damage to your mental state and nervous system, for the essence of the masculine is activity, aggression. Some great fear in childhood forced you to defend yourself, pushed you from your natural position and compelled you to adopt a defensive stance. That left the decisive scar in your mind.

You are on the defensive the whole time, constantly with-drawing. And that offers a logical explanation for all your behaviour: your 'alienation' from the masses, as you call it, your fear of the 'pointlessness' of the future, your revolt against exams, your attitude towards the city, the world in general and particularly women. In every circumstance you felt something that was unclear to you, filled you with fear and made you passive. It's pretty obvious that you were made passive by your mother, that she is responsible for your defensiveness. She's the one that 'taught' you, in the same way as she would bind a wound that was bleeding. In her you saw protection, the main sexual actor, so that all the initiative for sex remained with her. Even at the very beginning, your attitude to sexuality was the wrong way round, you remained passive. Since you got to know women in a very violent but also fearful way, that became the foundation of your mental development. Your will was always dormant. You were not an actor. You often told me how much of an influence nature had on you, how you succumbed to it, with pleasure even, as if in that way you would evade responsibility. You have always avoided making decisions! Or you didn't even avoid them, as you were simply incapable of making a decision. You were not living, you were being lived by nature, by events, chance. You simply did not recognise action as a consequence of the will. You recognised it only theoretically. That you stayed so long in the city was a barely discernible revolt against your male nature, which was still inside you, I'm sure about that. Your 'attacks' show that. I don't actually know why your desire for action came to the surface in such unusual forms, but it's probably because they were created by the circumstances in which you found yourself when the desire arose. It's clear that you didn't understand why this was happening. You said it might be sadism, but I'm sure it isn't. These are attacks of a suppressed organism seeking action.

That, it seems to me, is your problem. And there's only one solution. In your relationships with women you must become an actor. In that way you will help your suppressed male nature to free itself. I'm convinced that you will be transformed. You must create the feeling that you are the one with a woman at your disposal – that you are a man who has his own strength and will. Then you will acquire agency in your actions, as well as in your relation to the world. The difficulty is that you have to do all this yourself, no one else can do it for you. It's your decision. Your first decision. If your first decision is a rational one, under compulsion, it doesn't mean that the second won't be emotional...'

The inflow of nature: as if evading responsibility. Maybe he had indeed taken refuge in nature whenever he was afraid to make a decision. Taking new steps, yes, it was true, he had always feared that most of all. Emma, for instance... Each new woman meant a new step, a break with the well-trodden path. And he always sank into the material world before events that unfolded without his will. Hadn't even his mother sensed that? 'Haven't you found a woman yet? You should do... I'm old and... you were still young then... You really must find a woman... you should marry... Yes, you really must find one!'

His mother had said the same as Daria, only in different words. His mother sensed something was wrong. Their relationship changed. Not in essence, but it took on a new form. Their actions contained an unusual coldness that disturbed them both greatly, but which they were powerless to change. He felt that there was some kind of mistrust between them, a hidden shame. He was no longer a child, but a young man. He was constantly aware that he was living with his mother, he knew it was incest, and he was assailed by guilt. They both remained on the border of cold reason, they didn't dare to go further. His mother did not relax, she left the initiative to him, while he was not bothered by her passivity. He dared not even think about beating her now. And he was suddenly bothered by her unwashed body, which had a distinctive smell that disturbed him and was unpleasant to him. The whole time he was troubled by the fact that he had been born from the vagina that then became the object of his enjoyment. They both felt something was being destroyed and there was no way back. So the mistrust grew from one day to the next, the coldness permeated their relationship and they could no longer look each other in the eye. They began to fear their sexual bonding, but they still could not forego a single night – as if hoping that everything would somehow be resolved.

Such were these moments of his. A desperate struggle to dig out fragments of the past that had compelled him to return. And yet… He felt it was no longer there, that everything was different, that time had come in between… In his heart there arose a confused feeling that he had never experienced before. He felt as if he had done something reckless… Was that remorse? Yes, it was, he told himself. Maybe the real path was in the city, through the city. Certainly not a withdrawal into emptiness. For now it was clear! Daria had finally identified it. Passivity. Now he felt that his mother was the source… Did he still have any desire for her, had he imagined that he longed for the past, wasn't it just an excuse for his inability to decide and take action? For this coldness in bed with his mother: was that not repulsive, or only a desperate attempt to dig his way into the past and thus excuse his flight from the future? The act was no longer authentic, it must stop. There was mistake here, a dead point and Daria had said… become an actor, achieve the feeling that you have the will to take a woman, that you are the aggressor, that you are a man, that you don't withdraw! For only then would a flight from responsibility be impossible, and everything would change. How could someone rationally decide to do something that he otherwise would not consider? 'If your first decision is a rational one, it doesn't mean that the second won't be emotional,' wrote Daria. 'It all lies in the awareness that you can do it.'

Perhaps he did the right thing when he decided to wait in the beech wood for Polonka, the priest's niece. Perhaps the feeling of hopelessness would have remained if he hadn't seen her at the mass he had attended for reasons he did not understand. Daria's letter was the deciding factor, but with Polonka the possibility came nearer, became real.

She came along the path, carrying a large basket with two cans of milk and looking at the ground. She seemed to him plumper than a few days earlier, when he saw her at Geder's, perhaps because her short sleeves revealed much more of her arms. She was also wearing a different dress and looked more curvaceous and bulky. He sat back down on a tree root. She did not notice him until she saw his shadow falling on the path. Then she raised her eyes and gave a startled look. But her face immediately relaxed into a smile of relief:

'Oh, it's you! You gave me such a fright!'

'Do I look frightening?'

'I didn't imagine it was you. What are you doing here?'

'Waiting for you.'

She blanched. She didn't know how to interpret his words.

He noticed the change and was confused. He looked at the ground and poked at the moss with a piece of wood. If he moved too quickly it would all be over. She already sensed that something wasn't quite right.

'It's like this… When I was a child things happened that… had a negative influence on me… that put me in a strange position…'

'Ah…' she said with relief, as if the tension had passed.

'You know, my mother… I was very attached to her. And I was afraid of women, apart from her. I was afraid of them!'

She stared at him in surprise.

'Now I've discovered that it's all because of my passivity, my fear of making decisions. And now I need to decide. That I'm the one with power. The one that takes a woman. Do you understand?'

She was trembling.

'I'd like to… you know!'

It looked as if she was about to flee, so he jumped at her, knocked her over and grabbed her around the waist.

'You're a woman, aren't you? All women like to do it!'

She hit him in the face, grabbed his hair and pulled as hard as she could.

'I'll scream, I'll scream! I'll tell my uncle…'

'Be quiet, calm down!'

'No! I'll bite you… Help!'

He put his hand across her mouth. Her shout echoed through the woods, he froze. There was a path nearby, a field. If someone came… He pulled a knife from his pocket and waved the blade in front of her face. She turned to stone. When he saw she was overcome with horror he shuddered with the sense of his own power.

'If you move, I'll stick a knife in your throat! I once killed some puppies, the blood spurted everywhere!'

When he heard his own words he shuddered once more. Something was unleashed, a wave of associations, as if he had fallen from a cliff and slipped into the depths.

'And often I've wanted to grab hold of someone and smash them and beat them to death. In the city I beat a police officer to a pulp. That's action! Will! My will! I have strength!'

She was trembling, staring at him wide-eyed. When he waved the knife in front of her she followed it with her eyes. Her body shook in great spasms.

There were beads of sweat on her forehead.

'Now undress…'

She shook her head violently.

'Strip!' he hissed.

Tears ran from her eyes. He felt she was in his power, that she was succumbing to his will, his strength: he could do with her whatever he wanted. He became engorged, he grew, he felt proud and inflated. The blood pounded in his veins, he sensed the closeness of the act.

Then it all happened quickly, eagerly. Fear at his sudden transformation so disabled her that she acted mechanically, almost as if she were not present, she only trembled and shook in spasms. Whenever she showed too much daring or made a suspicious movement, he waved the knife at her and she turned to stone. He folded up her skirt to her breasts. She squeezed her legs together and did not want to open them. He flashed the knife and she went limp.

He saw that she had passed out.

He was alarmed. 'Polonka! … Polonka! … Don't do that!'

He shook her like a bunch of straw and slapped her cheeks. Then he sighed helplessly and kneeled over her. He saw that she had her eyes open and was moving. She was staring at his face.

He didn't get up, he was thrown to his feet. Crashing from tree to tree, he fell on the moss, picked himself up and staggered on. At the lower edge of the wood he lay down. On the road in the valley the evening bus was already running. Dusk was approaching, with small shadows that lay on the orchards and fields.

The church clock on the hill struck the hour. He failed to register how many times it struck…

Dusk finally came; it was dark, but there were a few stars and the moon was rising above the plain. Cold crept into his body. It got him moving, carrying him blindly across the fields towards the valley. Several times he tripped and fell, but he was carried forward relentlessly. Again the church clock struck the hour.

And again he was unaware how many times it struck. The stronger the feeling of guilt inside him, the more he felt the urge to move forward. A kind of silent scream, shock at what he had done and his own strength drove him on. He stopped by the vineyards and looked into the valley. Then he was overcome. A spasm of laughter burst from him, but was quickly torn. Again, he was driven across the fields. He felt in his pocket and found a lighter. Once again a hoarse laugh burst from his mouth.

Then he saw a house in front of him. It stood alone on the edge of the village, an orchard above it bounded by a hedge. He leaped forward, he was in the uncut grass, he was drawn downwards… There was the dung heap… There was no light in the yard… nor any dog dragging its chain… He felt compelled to go behind the house… the light was shining through the window among the plum trees… There the grass had been cut… He pulled out a lighter, flicked it on, moved closer… Flames burst forth. He was already running upwards through the orchard. He jumped over the hedge and then crossed the ploughed field to the right, towards the hill… His heart was pounding, he was gasping for breath, his lungs felt as if they might explode. He turned round. The flame was rushing across the dry straw, it moved above the house, flew along the ridge, slipped along the margins. Then it spread across the roof and burst into the air. It began to crackle. He heard someone shout:

'Fire!'

And then again: 'Fire! Klemar's is on fire!'

He rushed across fields and orchards. He tripped, rolling over on the lumpy earth. Then forward, to the trees, a copse. There he stopped, breathing heavily, fell on his knees, raking his hands through the cold, dewy grass and staring at the fire raging below him.

There was a racket in the village, dogs were going wild and breaking free from their chains. People ran around, grabbing buckets and filling them on the way. Thick white smoke churned into the sky. At the upper end of the valley a siren could be heard, drawing quickly nearer. He heard a roof beam crack and collapse.

He squatted there for a long time, watching.

Then he got up and continued towards the top of the hill. He was breathing excitedly. He felt a lightness near his heart, a kind of wild joy flowing through his veins like blood. Something had arisen within him, he felt like shouting. The shout was already in his throat, but then he had an attack of fright. The shout broke. He walked faster.

The voices of people shouting became more distant. He was nearing the top.

There, above the young wood, where the hill ended, stood a large tree stump. He went over to it and looked round. The flames had already died down, only the glowing lines of the half-burned roof beams showed him where the fire was. There was still the sound of barking, but far away, barely audible.

A refreshing chill bathed him. He leaned against the tree stump. The night was calming down. The mist shrouding the horizon to the south had dispersed. He could clearly see the shadow of the plain that flowed into the dark line of the horizon.

Then it was night, through which distant moments percolated. The moon rose above the plain, rounded and criss-crossed with dark shadows, and with a misty halo around it. On the edge of the wood he felt a pine tree, climbed its trunk, ran his hands over the bark. How rough it was in comparison with a beech, which was so smooth. And the meadows by the stream were silvery grey, weren't they? And this landscape, light and dark shadows, outlines, sharply bordered. And the night chill, splashing with the wind, horizontally, the dew rising into the air, the dewy grass. The outlines were sharp, very sharp, as if drawn in by an invisible marker. And the different hues. Every object was a different shade in the yellowish light. That was the moon, the golden moon! The meadow was pale, the wood darker, sharper. The greyish trunks, standing in line. Like a fence. He turned around. Those stars, that sand, that dust, who scattered it? And he turned again. The ranks of alders by the stream, the water pattering along the stream bed like water in a gutter...

When rain strikes a windowpane the sound is frightening. The same when it hits your face. Then you are washed, it runs over you, bites into your skin, it does not rattle, but it is damp, it smells of rain, a special, smoky smell; you reach out your hand into the rainy air, then stretch it out in front of you, a fluttering curtain, through it chimneys can hazily be seen and if you take hold of the wall it is hard, you can touch it, it's rough like bark, everything is rough; you have to lean your chest against it, then it is rough and wet, and the ground is rough; there's no real smoothness, it doesn't exist; surfaces, too, are rough... bring me a little water from the stream and pour it over me... you pour it and rub it in, you see and touch the smoothness, but you feel roughness, a negligible roughness... a little water in your hands... that hollowness, how it sounds as if it is coming from somewhere foggy, voices also retain a touch of roughness, especially if they come from the past; does time really fly past, the time that is no more?... To touch and to be distant, it's not good to be distant, that's no help, you can touch only from close up, bark for instance, and of course you don't touch a voice, but how it washes up from the past, it has to come in some way, there must be some connection... There's something else that needs to be done.

Geder's light is on…

He's still up.

What's he doing? Reading strange books, planing some wood. Lately, he has given up washing altogether. Daria always smelled of soap. In fact, there was a bad smell across the whole valley. When there were storms there was a pungent smell that tickled the throat. Here they don't bathe, sleeping and working in the same shirt for a month or more. Sweat. Geder's lights are on. Why is he up so late every night… his yard is littered with rubbish…

Will he hear knocking?

This room! It's colder than outside. The windows are small and dirty, the sun doesn't penetrate. How is that man living? The same way year after year. It's all still like it was when he was first here. An iron bed that still squeaks if you lean on it, but probably even more wobbly now. And the same green cover. There's the dusty stove and inside, the same old pots and pans, he certainly doesn't bake bread, he buys it at the baker's, and on top of the stove all sorts of jumble, books, newspapers, shoes, pieces of wood, cobwebs in the corner. Janek had never noticed these things before, only when he returned from a more ordered world did he see what had been right in front of his eyes since childhood, but had not bothered him. Now it was as if he was seeing everything for the first time. Was it, then, possible to return to the past? Does the past exist?

One of the small windows was ajar; he went closer and peeped inside. He saw Geder kneeling on the dirty floor by a wooden incubator.

'Oh little yellow eggs!' he was saying hoarsely. 'They'll be chickens! What am I saying? Turkeys!' He reached towards a tray on the ground, picked up the glass and drained it. The tray held a bottle of schnapps. He put the glass back and wiped his mouth.

'Brrr! Would you like a little schnapps, my chicky wickies? My little mousy wousies? Will you be out soon? Peck, peck, peck, out of the shell, here we are, cluck, cluck, cluck!'

Janek knocked on the window. Geder started and looked round. Then he grabbed the tray and pushed it under the bed. He dusted off his knees and went to open the door. When he saw Janek he looked startled, but then he opened his arms wide.

'There he is, our Janek Banek!'

'I've come to visit you,' said Janek drily.

'Of course. You've been away for two years. Do you remember? You sat on this bed the day you left. As sad as a felled tree.'

'Sad is the one who does the felling.'

'You always said things that I only half understood. Come in.'

He closed the door and led Janek to the main room.

'You're raising chickens?' Janek gestured towards the incubator.

'What about you, how are you?'

'What about you, how are you?' replied Janek.

'I've discovered something damned devilish!'

'That the chicken came before the egg?'

'That it wasn't my fault I was born!'

'I hope the guilty one is safely behind bars!' commented Janek.

'I'm not joking, damn it! Look! This,' he picked up a large wall clock from the table, 'and this,' he pulled a watch from his pocket, 'opened my eyes. The wall clock worked the whole time. Best clock in the world. This pocket watch dilly-dallied, the bitch, so that I felt like stepping on it and passing out with pleasure when it crunched under foot. So I reached for the pocket watch once when I went into town. Of course, it had stopped. I looked at the wall clock, to set the pocket watch – and damn it, the wall clock showed half past ten and the pocket watch half past ten as well! But the pocket watch had stopped!'

'It stopped at half past ten in the evening and you wanted to set it twenty-four hours later,' Janek observed.

'Good heavens, you're a clever one! Two years studying and look what it's made of you!'

'Absolutely nothing,' replied Janek.

'But listen: a week later and exactly the same thing happens! But at a different time. A quarter to twelve. And a few days ago exactly at twelve! Now I'm thinking: it's happened three times in two weeks that I reach for my pocket watch twenty-four hours after it stopped!' Janek was walking restlessly round the room. 'Yes, it happens, it happens.'

'Wait a sec!' Geder put his hand on his arm. 'Yesterday I was rewinding my watch and it broke. Goodbye forever. But the wall clock, it stopped right at the same moment, exactly when I broke the pocket watch, all on its own!'

'They had an agreement.'

'Janek, I want you to be serious. Take this example. Charlemagne died in the year 814.'

'And?' said Janek with a shrug.

'814 is the code for my bike lock.'

'A historical conspiracy!'

'What's more, 814 is my house number!'

'A geographical conspiracy!'

'And last of all, and this is the real devil: 814 is my birth date. The 14th of the 8th. What do you say to that!'

Janek walked round the room once more. 'You're becoming an oddball!'

'You think it's a joke? Let me show you something.'

From beneath the bed he pulled a large piece of cardboard with an ovum drawn in the centre and around it a mass of sperm. 'Look. This in the middle, you know what it is. And all around are the male whatnots that spurt from you when you do it with a woman. Millions of them. And of all these millions, only one fertilises the egg. Just one! And I wonder: how is it that from all these, it was me as I am that was made? Why aren't I my brother and why isn't my brother me?'

'What about death, Geder?'

For some time Geder stared in silence at the ovum on the card-board. 'What?'

'Are you afraid?'

'I'm talking about life, Janek... Are you sick?'

'Everything I see around me is sick. Everything I smell. Everything I can touch. Everything beyond the horizon and everything inside me, so close that it's too close.'

After a short pause he gave a sour smile. 'Interesting, this student humour. By the way, did you know the Klemars' house burned down?'

'I heard.'

'They say someone started a fire.'

'I'm not surprised.'

'And the priest's niece, Polonka. Did you hear what happened?'

'She got married?'

'Someone raped her. She won't say who. The priest sent her back to her parents, although she didn't want to go because her step-father was cruel to her. The train stopped on the bridge above the Mura. She opened the door and jumped into the river. Five hundred metres downstream they pulled her body out, drowned.'

'Evidently she didn't know how to swim,' said Janek with a shrug.

'You used to have more feeling for other people. Ljubljana has changed you.'

'Why did your wife run off, Geder?'

Geder took a deep breath and stared at the ceiling. 'Janek, there are certain things I'd rather we didn't talk about.'

'The word in the parish is that you beat her on the naked arse with a cudgel.'

'What they say in the parish is not worth two hoots.'

'Some say that you can't get it up anymore.'

'Some are under the devil's influence.'

'Matajko claims that your thing was cut off when you were little.'

'Matajko? A hundred years ago he'd have had to show me some respect!'

'The parish doesn't respect you.'

'I respect the parish even less!'

'You go around saying that farmers are manure.'

'The more you dig it, the more it smells.'

'The farmers say you are an even bigger shitheap. That your house is falling down around your ears.'

'It's still standing.'

'That if you want to slaughter a pig you have to buy one, because you don't have your own.'

'No, because I'm not a farmer.'

'Your fields are full of weeds.'

'Those who say that are growing only nettles behind the shithouse!'

'You go around unwashed, they say.'

'And they bathe every day – in slurry!'

'It seems they'd like to get rid of you.'

'Janek! I'll tell you this – may the devil strike me dead – I'm the most normal person in this parish! I've read books and I know all too damn well what the world is like. The priest – no offence – likes to spread fear from the pulpit. And you, too, are not without your oddities – again, no offence. It's said that you and your mother – thank God the priest knows nothing about this – that you and your mother…'

Janek grabbed hold of a chair and raised it above Geder's head.

'Give me the chair,' said Geder, unperturbed.

'Never, ever let anything like that cross your tongue again!'

'Give me the chair, Janek. I'm not accusing you of anything –'

The door suddenly opened and Janek's mother stood on the doorstep.

'Holy mother of God!' She opened her arms wide. 'Janek!' She erupted into hysterical tears and slid to her knees.

Janek put the chair down and went over to her. 'Are you spying on me?'

'I didn't know you were here.'

'So why did you come?' he raised his voice.

She pointed at Geder. 'I clean for him. He's on his own.'

'Poor thing!'

'He wouldn't give money for you otherwise,' she said by way of apology.

'He stopped giving money two years ago! Since then it's the council.'

'Yes, but he did before, for the grammar school…'

'Haven't you paid off that small change after two years?'

'But he's got no one –'

'What do you do for him?' roared Janek. 'Feed his frogs? His lizards? Wash his underpants? Sweep the chicken shit from the house?'

Aranka bowed her head. 'Oh, Janek…'

'Oh, Janek. Oh, Janek.' He mocked her. He went over to Geder with a grin on his face. 'Oh, Janek. Oh, Janek.'

He let the door slam as he left. Outside, he stopped and eaves-dropped at the slightly open window.

'Lojz, you promised you wouldn't quarrel with him!' he heard his mother say.

'Hold your tongue, woman,' replied Geder edgily.

'You must have said something to him to make him like that!'

'Yes, that he's whoring around with you, that's what I said!' snapped Geder.

'Loooojz – '

'That's not my name!'

'Did you say anything about us?'

'And what would I say about us?'

'You know.'

'That we've both had you. That you cheated on him with me and on me with him? You gypsy whore. You robbed me blind. I paid for him, I fed you and him both – it's surprising I've still got a shirt on my back! And all because you bewitched me, you went on your knees and said: "I'll bear you a child, Lojz, I'll bear you a son, Lojz" – damn the name – never call me that again! Never again! And what have you given me after five years! Fuck all!'

'Loooojz –'

'I'm not Lojz! From today I'm Geder to you. Geder! It's over! I'm not a fool! And you're fat. Fat and barren. All women are barren!'

He fell to the floor beside the incubator and put his hands to his face.

'I'll wash your clothes,' said Aranka calmly. 'Or I'll sweep up. It's a bit of a mess. I'll sweep up.'

Geder said nothing. Aranka put down the basket that she had been holding the whole time, went into a side room, returned with a broom and began sweeping. From time to time she looked at Geder. He raised his head and looked at her. Then he went to her.

'Aranka. I'm sorry. I'm not a violent man.'

Aranka took hold of his sleeve. 'Did you tell him about us?'

'No,' said Geder, shaking off her hand.

'I was so afraid!'

'But one thing is true, or the devil take me. In five years, nothing!'

'What if it's not me...'

'Your son is fertile but he didn't impregnate you! We've both spurted inside you and what has come of it?'

'You've had so many women and it didn't work with any of them...'

'Because they're all barren!' yelled Geder, turning and putting his head in his hands. His shoulders shook.

Aranka reached out a hand to touch him, but at the last moment thought better of it. 'Maybe soon...'

'Soon?' said Geder angrily. 'You want to steal more from me? Geder may be odd, but he's no fool!'

'Loooojz ...'

'I know what I'm going to do! Find a real woman! One that isn't a worthless piece of shit. One dripping from the eyes and mouth.'

'Loooojz ...'

Geder leaped towards her, snatched the broom from her, grabbed the basket and tried to pull it from her hands, then thought better of it, fell to his knees, reached under the bed, pulled out a crate of potatoes, poured some into the basket, shoved it into her hands and then pushed her towards the door.

He pushed her outside and slammed the door. Aranka banged on it.

'Lojz, please...'

She burst into hysterical tears.

Geder stood on the other side of the door, his legs apart, like an animal getting ready for a fight.

'I'll jump on your stomach!'

Concealed behind the woodshed against the wall beside the door, Janek could see both of them: Geder through the window and, in the semi-darkness, his mother before the door. Her crying decreased, she turned slowly and went into the darkness.

Inside, Geder was pacing up and down. At one point, he went through a side door and reappeared with a white shirt and black boots. He took off his shirt, took a small bottle of eau de cologne from a drawer and rubbed it across his chest and under his arms. Then he sniffed his hands.

'I'll find a woman! Now or never!' He put on the white shirt, buttoning it carefully. Sitting on the edge of the bed, he put on some polished high boots. 'Jesus! I will not be the only man in this village without children!'

He got up, reached for his cap, put it on, and smoothed his hair and moustache. Then he headed determinedly towards the door. But the next moment he stopped and stared at the floor. He raised his head and stared into space for a while. He staggered over to the chair and literally sank onto it, putting his face in his hands. In the distance, a church clock struck a late hour. Geder bent down and began to remove his boots.

Janek became aware that his mother was once more approaching the door from the darkness. She banged on it and twice called out: 'Lojz!'

Geder got up, went to the door and opened it. Aranka pushed past him into the room.

'Lojz…'

Geder sat back down on the chair. Aranka sank to the floor in front of him and took his hand.

'Lojz…'

'Stop it.'

'There's something I must tell you.'

'Everything's been said already.'

'Some good news!' She reached for his hand and pressed it on her stomach. 'Can you feel it?'

'Yes, your stomach.'

'It's bloated.'

'Because you're fat. It's all the food I've given you.'

'Lojz, it's there!'

Geder became agitated: 'What?'

'A baby!' cried Aranka, half in tears. 'A baby!'

Geder jumped up, grabbed her shoulder and pulled her to her feet. 'Five minutes ago nothing, and now suddenly this? Did the devil impregnate you outside.'

'Lojz,' said Aranka calmly, 'before I didn't know.'

'And how do you know now?'

'It moved! It's moving! A woman knows when there's a baby inside her.'

'If you are lying, I'll kill you!'

Aranka burst into tears. 'It's there, Lojz, it's there!'

'It's moving?' Geder began to laugh wildly. 'It's moving!' He planted Aranka on a chair and kneeled in front of her. 'You sit here. Don't move! I want to watch you. An hour.'

Aranka smiled vainly, took off her headscarf and let down her wild black hair. Geder was as happy as a child. 'Heavens, you're beautiful! A mother. The mother of my child. I'll start believing in God!'

Late that night, when his mother was sleeping, he took the axe from the nail by the door and went towards the chestnut tree on the rise above the woods. The moonlight showed him the way. He began to strike at the trunk close to the ground. The chestnut was so high that he could barely see its crown. The sky suddenly clouded over, but because he had been hacking at the tree for quite some time, covered in sweat, and the tree had still not begun to fall, he noticed nothing but the chips of wood that were flying in all directions and the axe that was threatening to slip from his sweaty hands. When he stopped, panting, to take a rest, it immediately seemed strange to him that above the large valley to his left there was a strange darkness tinged with red. It was equally dark to his right, where the stream ran through the valley. He looked at the sky and saw black clouds gathering. Then he was blinded by a sudden flash that shot to the edge of the valley, and then another and another, while at the same time it thundered, rolling to the invisible horizon with such force that the ground beneath his feet trembled slightly. And in an instant the wind was there, rushing in so that the tree groaned. Fat drops of rain were falling and there was a whooshing sound as if water was rushing in from somewhere. Janek resumed his task, swinging the axe as if his life depended on it, for he knew that the wind would help him. Again there was a flash of lightning, this time right above him, and a fierce storm poured down on him, so that in a moment he was soaked to the skin. Suddenly there was a large crack and the giant tree began to fall. He jumped out of the way, the crown of the tree sank into the bushes that grew on the gentle slope and the lower part of the trunk was thrown into the air, then all was still. Lightning illuminated the slope and in the blinding light he saw that the chestnut was unbelievably big, its crown lay so far away that he could barely see it. He pushed his way through the bushes. And then he could finally touch what he wanted: the chestnut leaves. They were softer than he expected, but hard enough to weave a chestnut garland from them. The time had come. The pain he felt when he heard what his mother told Geder reached its peak.

The valley was gripped by alarm. People were knocking on the priest's door and demanding that he declare a miracle or the devil's work. An explanation was required; people were scared. But the priest did not speak out until mass on Sunday, from the pulpit:

'As the prophet Isaiah said – and there's no reason to disbelieve him, for he was a prophet – God,' and here he raised his finger, "will empty the surface of the Earth, cleave it in two and scatter its inhabitants on all sides." And then,' he paused and raised his voice, 'it will be the same for God's servants and for ordinary people, for masters and slaves, for creditors and debtors, for farmers and gypsies! In the Last Judgement, God will not distinguish between you and me, his servant. That is what I lay upon your heart. There is no difference between you and me. Except that I am closer to God. And I am authorised – yes, authorised, that is a word you understand – to tend to his flock on Earth. You are his flock and you act like one!' He calmed down slightly. 'What shall we say about the chestnut tree? I know what you expect of me. That I declare a miracle! But that, my dear parishioners, I will not do! According to our grandmothers, the chestnut stood on that hill for at least six hundred years. I will not say that is a lie. But certainly six hundred years ago, if not before, the sinful story arose that the chestnut tree was sacred. That if an unworthy human hand should harm it, a great misfortune will befall this place, this parish. That, my dear parishioners, is an old wives' tale. And old wives' tales are as far from belief in God as your hair is from the sole of your foot. I'm not saying that I did not help to perpetuate it. You paid for masses for the chestnut tree, you asked me to pray for it, to bless it. I did so because I did not want to wound you in your simplicity. May God forgive me.' He wiped the sweat from his brow. 'The thing you prayed would not happen has now happened! The chestnut is no more! And because of that you came as a flock before God's altar. You have been driven by fear. You are convinced that evil will now follow. Now the first seal will be broken, and the second seal and the third seal, and a white horse with a black killer, and a red horse will appear and its rider will swing a gigantic sword, and a third horse will appear and its rider will carry a pair of scales. But as your spiritual pastor I tell you that this fear is stuff and nonsense!' He leaned back and raised his head. 'The old chestnut is no more. Someone cut it down, all right. He must have had a hard time, because it was as big as five ordinary trees. However! Does anyone among you,' he pointed at his audience, 'know who committed this sinful act? For this is the work of a man, since only men use axes, and it is completely clear that the chestnut tree was cut down by one of you. One of you,' he pointed at the congregation. 'Someone who is not entirely in his right mind. Someone who is, and I intend no offence, a little mad. However... is there one among you that we could say is not of sound mind? I would not dare to accuse anyone. That would immediately expose him to the contempt and mockery of the rest, which would not be a Christian thing to do. And to accuse all of you would be unwise. This unfortunate matter of the chestnut tree is one of those things that only God understands, and so it is his business to do something about it. The only thing that we can do is to pray. And that we shall do. All kneel. Repeat after me.' He put his hands together. 'Our Father, which art in heaven...'

Towards evening, with the sun already sinking behind the hills, Janek approached Geder's house. As usual, he first stopped at the window next to the woodshed and peeped inside. He saw that Geder was sitting on the edge of the bed, polishing his shoes. He saw that when he had finished he put them on his bare feet. He took a mirror down from the wall and leaned it against the edge of the bed. He turned round in front of it, looking at his footwear from every angle. He seemed satisfied. Janek opened the door and went in.

Geder was startled. 'I didn't hear you knock!'

'Neither did I.'

Geder picked up the mirror and hung it back on the wall. 'I was giving my boots a polish. I'm going into town to do a few errands.'

'Geder, it's June and those are winter boots.'

'I'm used to a firm grip. In shoes your feet spread too much. Like walking through mud.' Suddenly he looked more closely at Janek. 'What have you got on your head?'

'A crown of chestnut leaves.'

'You think you're a king, or what?'

'When a sacred tree falls, some of us must take on a saintly shine.'

'Sacred tree, oh come on. Someone needed firewood.'

'The chestnut is still lying where it fell.'

'They'll come eventually and chop it up, and take it away. I know how the peasant mind works.'

He turned and took his boots through the side door. He returned with a loaf of bread and a long knife and put both on the table.

'Help yourself, go on.'

Janek reached for the knife, turned it in his hand and examined it. 'When I was a kid, my father and I often slept in the woods. Once I found him beside me with a knife like this in his neck.'

'Didn't your father ride off on his old nag and never return?'

'We were selling pigs at the market. My old man said: five thousand. The buyer said: are you mad? And he went off. Then my dad picked up a bag and went after him. Four and a half, he said, and the bag as well. The buyer hands over the money, takes the bag and leaves. When he gets home he opens the bag, and guess what's in it? Me. I jump out, pull it from his hands and rush off home.'

'What you gypsies come up with!'

'But gypsy women are all right, eh?'

Geder looked awkward. 'It depends on the individual.'

'My mother has twenty children. They're all doctors, apart from one, who is a patient. That's me.'

'Why don't we go outside, in the light?'

'Tell me something, Geder. How was it the first time you lay with a woman?'

'Wait a minute,' Geder began to fidget. 'You want to talk about that?'

'That's right. I want to talk about that. Tell me.'

'Well, you know… It draws it out of you, doesn't it? You erupt. It does you good.'

'I didn't enjoy it.'

Janek sat on the edge of the bed and stared into the distance. He spoke as if telling himself a story.

'I remember the night. The moon in the sky. A full, curious eye. I could smell the coldness of the night. That was the damp coming from the valley. A fox barked in the woods. I could feel the wind licking the earth on the fields. I could feel the roughness of the fox's coat and the hoarseness of its voice. I could feel the mossy ground beneath its paws. I could smell the tree resin, the spruce needles, fallen branches. The warm feathers of a magpie. The wood nearby. I could smell my skin, sweat. The water smelled of mud. And acorns. And the coldness travelled over my skin. Shivering. A feeling came over me that I should go, drag myself like an animal to the fire or a den. I ended up in the house. In the darkness. But the moon was shining. There were stripes of moonlight across the floor. I peered into the corner and there it was. On the mattress, lit by moonlight. A half-naked body. The stomach gleaming like a meadow. I heard breathing. Then… the chill came after me. And fear. Once again I had the urge to drag myself to a den. I got a hard-on. I felt the smoothness of skin. And warmth. Warmth. And then she opened up! I sank into her. With a cry. A yell. Then – there was gasping. The spasm passed. And I was there. In the moonlight I saw only myself. Naked. I smelled. I smelled odd. The chill returned… I passed out.'

Geder was silent. After some time he managed one word: 'Strange.'

'That night… The wind was blowing. It was thundering. Something inside me began to decay. To rot like leaves. I was cheated. In the morning she was sitting beside me. Exhausted. Taciturn. Scared. She reached out her hand to comfort me. Then there rose inside me… as if… as if… Blood came to my mouth. Fire in my chest. I ran out and grabbed hold of a pine tree. Rain was pouring down. I raised my face to it.'

He got up, went to the window on the other side of the bed and stared out across the valley.

'Never mind that, Janek …'

'How light the sky is at the horizon!'

'No one is without a wound.'

'I have no wounds. I've burned out. What I've been doing the last six months is just smoke from my fireplace. The fire's gone out.' He turned and moved to the centre of the room. He began to beat his chest. 'And what did that fire create? It created smoke. Smoke, which is lost in the unlit place. Up there! And down there! Nothing!'

'Janek …'

Janek turned to the window and once more looked across the valley. 'How light the sky is at the horizon!' He turned around. 'Are you superstitious, Geder?'

'You know I'm not.'

'Me neither. But look at that light! Full of decaying leaves.' He sat on the other side of the bed and stared into space. 'Autumn has always been inside me. Somewhere above my stomach. A desire to be extinguished.'

'Let's go and have a talk with the priest. I wanted to go and see him anyway.'

'No, we're staying here.'

'God, there is something wrong with you.'

Janek got up and approached Geder. 'Hit me.'

Geder shifted restlessly. 'You're really going crazy.'

'Hit me!'

'My boy!'

'If you don't hit me I'll hit you.'

'Why?'

Janek punched him in the face. Geder responded instinctively and hit Janek hard on the head.

He was immediately sorry. 'Janek, I didn't mean it…'

'Now, Geder, all the bonds between us are torn. We are friends no more! Never again!'

'I'll be damned if I understand you.'

Janek grabbed the kitchen knife and thrust it towards Geder. 'Sit down. I'll say it again. Sit down.'

Geder moved backwards to the chair and sat down.

Janek waved the knife. 'I discovered, Geder, that you are a bitch! Are you hot? If you are, take off your shirt. I won't look at your sunken ribs. Is there anything I can get you? A glass of water, wine, schnapps, a piece of bread?'

'Listen, lad…'

'Shut up!' Janek waved the knife again. 'Who asked you to pay my school fees?'

'Your mother, who else?'

'How did she repay you?'

'Did my washing. Cleaned. A bit of gardening.'

'And?'

Geder was becoming increasingly confused. 'Janek, this is getting us nowhere.'

'Did she take her skirt off? Offer herself to you?'

'Janek, I've no idea what you're on about.'

'You're lying.'

'If you believe shitty peasants…'

'She told me herself.'

After a long silence, Geder said: 'Stupid cow!'

'Still lying?'

'If she told you herself then, the devil take me, I don't see why I should drag her from the shit.'

'You're deep in shit, too.'

'I am clean!'

'Like your underpants.'

'Don't accuse me, lad. Two years I paid for your education. And before that, at secondary school…'

'You're worse than all the yokels down there! They believe in old wives' tales, you believe in frogs!'

'And you're a gypsy! Sorry.'

'Lizards, chickens, frogs! Is that all you can manage – frogs?'

'What about you? Why did you come back? They threw you out. Because you're not clever enough. They showed you the door!'

'My home is here, in this village. I have to finish my degree here.'

'The money I wasted on you! And for what? A barefoot, ragged, dishevelled shit! How much money!'

'You paid for your whore.'

Geder raised his hand. 'Don't talk of her like that!'

'You're defending her!' Janek thrust the knife through the air close to Geder. 'You defend her? I'm the only one who can, me!' He beat his left hand against his chest. 'I'm the only one who can defend her, because she's mine! She was never yours! You stole her from me! You wanted everything for yourself. Because your seed is no good, you wanted everything! Chickens!' He kicked the incubator, which broke into pieces that scattered round the room. 'Where did you do it with her – here, on this filthy bed? On this creaking bed? Or outside, in the woods? But,' he stopped right in front of Geder, 'what you really want you can't have. A child! The only children you'll have are chickens!'

'Your mother is carrying it!' Geder stood up and went on the offensive. 'My child.'

Janek replied unusually calmly. 'My mother?'

'She told me yesterday.'

'She told you yesterday?'

'I wanted to spare you, but you gave me no choice.'

'There's no child, Geder.'

'There is.'

'Are you deaf, or do you not want to hear? There's no child!'

'How do you know?' yelled Geder, close to despair.

'A child would change your life, wouldn't it? Wouldn't it? But as an educated person – and you paid for most of my education in order to get access to the mother who brought me into this world – as an educated person I can assure you that there is no child. Because there cannot be. She had it cut out of her. When she gave birth to me, they removed her uterus because of an inflammation. So where is your child growing? In her large intestine?'

Geder staggered to the chair, sank onto it and crumpled.

'But… she told me yesterday.'

'Never believe a gypsy.' He leaned over Geder and hissed: 'You took her from me! You dead slime! You worthless piece of shit!'

Geder gave a hoarse moan. Janek watched him for some time. Then he went to the door. From there, he looked at him once more. Then he left, closing the door behind him.

He sneaked a last look into the room through the window by the woodshed.

G eder was staring into space. He looked deadly tired. Then he got up and went through the side door. He returned with his boots, sat on the bed and began to put them on. This time, he put socks on first. His movements became an unusual ritual, at first slow and hesitant, but then increasingly certain. When he had his boots on, he bent over and picked up the pieces of glass and the remnants of the incubator that Janek's kick had scattered round the room. He put them in a heap next to the bed. Then he went to the bookshelf and took all the books – there were about thirty of them – and threw them in a heap in the middle of the room. He took the clock off the wall and threw it on the heap, too. From beneath the bed he pulled a stack of old newspapers and added them. He collected everything in the room that could be moved, apart from the table and the bed, and put them on the heap. He picked up the knife and put it on the table. He went over to the mirror and looked at himself for a while. Then he took the mirror down and that also went on the heap. He pulled the cover off the bed and placed it over everything that he had heaped up. He went into the side room and came back with a whetstone for sharpening a scythe. He picked up the knife, sat on the bed and began to sharpen it. He raised the knife and looked at it from every angle. The setting sun shone on the blade through the window. Geder got off the bed and sat cross-legged on the floor. He unbuttoned his shirt and exposed his chest. He reached for the knife and with a hoarse cry plunged it into his heart. His body slumped forward.

The door opened and Janek, still wearing the chestnut leaf crown, rushed over to Geder and grabbed his shoulder. Geder fell back and collapsed onto the floor.

'Geder!' yelled Janek. He took hold of the knife and pulled it from Geder's chest.

'Geder!' he yelled hoarsely once more as loud as he could, with a mixture of accusation, pleading, atonement and despair.

But Geder did not move.

Janek stared at the bloody knife in his hand.

The police came and with them the investigating judge, a middle-aged man with a moustache and a hat. Janek didn't know what he would be asked and even less what he would answer. The judge did not look very sophisticated, but his first words showed that he was Janek's equal.

'What have we got here?' he asked as he walked slowly around Geder's body. 'In the midst of a society based on Reason there is a dark stain of Unreason. A dark, cancerous growth that threatens metastasis. If we do not remain constantly on our guard, it will grow and suffocate us all. So what is our duty? That we excise every manifestation of Unreason as soon as it appears. That we cut out, break down or isolate every malignant metastasis, however small, as soon as we identify it. Am I wrong in seeing in you such a metastasis? I think not. If I must, as investigating judge, play the role of surgeon, I won't resist. I am grateful for the duties laid upon me by my profession. If there are rats among us, then pest control is noble, even romantic work. Wouldn't you agree?'

He went over to the body, removed the crown of chestnut leaves from its head, looked at it and turned to Janek. 'I have the feeling that we'll find your fingerprints on these leaves. Am I wrong?'

Janek pulled the crown from his hand, put it on his head, went to the door and shouted: 'I hear the devil with trumpets! Out of the way! The army of gypsy demons is coming!'

From the door he marched to the body like a soldier. 'One – two – one – two – no one knows – what's happening here! Here comes – the black devil – who is feared – by all!'

He stopped, removed the chestnut leaf crown and raised it before him, as in prayer.

'A chestnut leaf crown. Woven on the fifth day after the fall of the tree that required five hours sweat.' He placed the crown on the floor in front of him. 'In my pocket five toads of medium size. I'll throw them over my head into the stream behind me.'

Five times he reached into his pocket and made as if he was throwing something over his head.

'One, two, three, four, five!' He turned and shouted: 'Heeey! Melalo! All the toads in the stream! Two on the left, two on the right, one in the middle. Now the crown!'

He picked up the chestnut leaf crown and once more placed it on his head. 'I'll dance three devilish dances. Melalo! You are a worm with a hundred heads, I know you! If you're a magpie, I know you! If you're a bark beetle, I know you. I know you in all your hundred forms!'

He took two steps back and yelled so loud that all those present started.

'Me-la-lo! Here I am, your son without reason. Play!'

Although they did not hear, all those present got the impression that the lively music of a hundred violins had started up somewhere. Janek whirled in a grotesque dance, flinging out his arms and legs, thrusting his head from side to side. Then it was as if the music stopped and Janek slumped to the floor, out of breath. He got up and yelled: 'Again!'

The dance was repeated. Janek caught his breath for a while, then he shouted: 'For the third time!'

The dance, almost the same as the first two times, was repeated. At the end Janek collapsed in a heap, gasping for breath.

The judge bent over and removed the crown from his head. 'Five hours swinging an axe for some woven leaves. Why?'

'That was the way the gypsies healed… lunatics,' panted Janek in reply.

'But why chop down a tree for some leaves that you could take from a branch?'

'For the parts to work, the whole must die.'

'And how does this chestnut leaf crown work?' asked the judge.

'It draws poison from the brain. It kills the worms that tunnel beneath the skull.'

'Should I believe you?'

'Put it on your head and you'll see.'

The investigating judge took a step towards Geder's body. 'I wouldn't like to end up like this gentleman here. The chestnut leaf crown evidently does more than draw poison from the brain. It can pierce your heart with a kitchen knife.'

He turned to Janek and shouted: 'Can't it?'

'For so long you don't use bad words,' Janek began to recite in a slightly poetic rhythm 'For so long you don't see things as they are, but the colour they were painted in the past. But then you slip on these smooth colours of your supposed forebears, you fall and break off a flake of paint. Beneath is something different, something completely different. You're disappointed at the false coloured beauty, at the stunning pastel shades, at the red sunset clouds. You are gripped by fury and peel off the paint, plane it off the trees, the sky, the woods, the faces – and finally into your hands flows the naked world, finally the naked world.'

The judge leaned towards him and in a neutral voice asked: 'Why did you kill him?'

'The moon shines, the hammer strikes, bum, bu-bum, bu-bum!' replied Janek in a similar tone. 'The grey cat goes into the birch wood. Bum, bu-bum, bu-bum!'

The priest, who the whole time had stayed discreetly in the background, now drew near. 'Janek, tell him the truth. He did not come here to harm you, he's just doing his job. Just as I must satisfy God, he must satisfy justice. God knows exactly what happened, you cannot fool him. You can fool us for a while, but what do you gain from that, except the feeling that you know how to lie convincingly?'

'Father, you don't speak in the name of God. You speak in the name of the Church.'

'I don't expect gratitude. What I gave, I gave freely, I don't accuse you. But don't forget you grew up in my house! You spent more time there than with the gypsies. I bought you clothes. You read my books. I taught you. And never, absolutely never was there any pretence between us. But now,' he suddenly raised his voice, 'I no longer know you! You come here, abandoning your studies after two years, and what do you do? You take an axe and you chop down the sacred chestnut tree and set alight this God forsaken parish! Did you think that in that way you'd kill off the superstition? My dear boy, I've been trying for thirty years, not to kill, but to ease this blindness. But not only can I not ease it – it is increasing!'

He turned to the body. 'And then Geder. He paid for your schooling, sent you money. Helped your mother, so she didn't starve. The harder I try, the less I understand what could have taken you so far. You were healthy, clever, you had a future. You had opportunities that few of your race enjoy. And now this!'

'And now this,' repeated Janek.

'I'm almost convinced a woman is to blame.'

'A woman,' the investigating judge continued. 'A man's life, whether old or young, all revolves around a woman, doesn't it? In my case too; I'm no exception. The only difference is that I would not kill because of a woman. Well, to be precise, I should say that until now I have not killed. Who knows, perhaps I could. Perhaps I even might. We don't know each other well enough to know what we're capable of. We can only go on what we've already done. Then probably we can only be amazed that we have done something that we were convinced was not in our nature. Isn't that right?'

'The sun rises like a dark ball,' Janek began to recite, 'so you give wings to a stone and drive it across the sea to measure the reach of your hand. It sinks behind the nearby rocks – the further you throw it, the closer it falls. So you turn and run, you would like to return to the womb beside the long dirty river that is your life, to go like lightning along its paths, but only the light shines from the night and returns to the night, and you remain where you are. Like when you step in a puddle and the water ripples all around your foot, in other words nowhere. Is that life? Or is that just my life?'

'When I was young, I also wrote poems,' said the judge, after a short silence. 'I think they were even better than yours, they rhymed. And they were more understandable. Simple, like me. Your letters are easier to understand than your poems.'

From his pocket he pulled a sheaf of letters, opened one and read: "'It's my second year here and the whole time I've felt a longing to return home; but longing is not the right word, it's more an urge – wild, bloody…"'

Janek leapt up and tried to pull the letters from his hand.

'Where did you get that?'

The judge moved the letter out of the way and warned Janek that there were two police officers outside the door.

'Did she give you the letters? Traitor! I should have wrung her neck.'

'Good job you didn't, because then I'd be investigating two murders.'

'You're not investigating, you are representing the profession that I did not manage to join. You have already condemned me.'

'Not I, my dear failed law student. But some determined prosecutor could cite words from this letter in court and add: As we can see, the accused recognised his own criminal instincts, which he fought against, but eventually succumbed to. Especially if we add the following words from the letters.' He unfolded another one and read: "From the very beginning, something has been driving me back home. And although the 'me' from the past was tormenting me, it was becoming stronger, tying my hands, dragging me back, as if that 'me', wherever it was, had not settled all its scores."'

He folded the letter and put it back in his pocket along with the others. 'In short, you abandoned your studies and returned to this remote village to settle scores. Is that not so?'

'That's right,' replied Janek tepidly. He appeared to be elsewhere, in another world.

'Do you have the feeling that you are responsible for your actions? Or that you are not? Or that you are one thing and your actions something else? Many criminals have thought like that.'

'Really?' sneered Janek.

'Some say they were merely following orders or instructions. Perhaps that's how it is with you. Perhaps you hear voices, have visions that are outside your consciousness. Perhaps a secret voice is whispering to you: Stab, strangle, dispose of, take revenge. Is that possible?'

Janek remained silent.

'I made some enquiries among your schoolmates and acquaintances. I never go into the field unprepared. And what did I find out? Some interesting facts. How you once slapped a professor. She asked you for a dance at a faculty party and you hit her. And then an incident in the theatre, where you went with some colleagues to see… wait a moment… Sophocles' Oedipus. In the middle of the performance you began to shout as if you were being murdered. The performance had to be stopped and you were dragged to the police station, where you were beaten.'

'I was not!'

'No, you beat them. You snatched the truncheon from one of the officers and before the astonished eyes of the others, beat him unconscious. How did you feel after that incident? I'm interested. Were you relieved, did you feel proud of yourself, did you feel important? A feeling you had achieved something? Or did you feel regret? Perhaps horrified by your actions? Tell me. I'm interested.'

Janek said nothing.

'I'd like to be your friend. I could simply stick handcuffs on you and have you taken off to jail: I'd be breaking no rules, it would be entirely lawful. Any other investigating judge would have done it long ago. I am different. A special case. I want to know. It's not enough to know that a criminal offence occurred, I want to know the reasons. Perhaps I know them already. But I'd like to hear them from you.'

'Na janav ko dad mro has!'

'Sorry?'

'Niko malen mange has! Miro gule daj merdijas! Pirani man pregelijas!'

'I'm too old to start learning a new language,' said the judge.

'Demons, demons!' screamed Janek. 'Away!'

He crawled on all fours about the room, scratching at the wooden floor like a dog.

'I want to get in! I need a den! Light, be extinguished!'

Janek lay on his back for some time, gasping as if short of breath. Then he put the chestnut leaf crown on his head and shouted: 'Memory, you are a demon! I know you, your name is Poreskoro! You have four cat heads and four dog heads and your tail is a snake with a poisonous tooth. You are a hermaphrodite. You fertilise yourself.'

He raised his voice: 'But I will kill you! I'll extinguish you! I'll spend the rest of my life in my den. I didn't see you, golden toad, I'd like to see you, golden toad. I know what you are. You are a female organ! At night you hop around and have fun! You are a female organ that each night is transformed into an animal! I know you! IdidntseeyouIdliketoseeyou! Kill my memory! Don't be afraid! Come! And kill my memory!'

'Since you are unwilling to talk to me,' said the judge after a long silence, 'I am compelled to form my own opinion about you. Including how you see yourself. It seems to me that you see yourself as better and higher than others. Correct me if I'm wrong. Whenever you like, at any point, you can interrupt me and say: You are wrong. I'll be glad of your corrections. It seems to me that you see society as a worthless mill that grinds down the individual into worthless dust. Isn't that so? Please respond. Show me that I'm wrong. Show me that I am not dealing with a dangerous, solitary, conceited criminal, who has excluded himself from society. Excluded himself because it did not immediately give him what he demanded. For a feature of this criminal is he does not expect, he does not expend energy, but he demands. And when he does not get what he wants, he raises his sense of grievance into some kind of quasi-philosophy.'

The judge once more pulled some papers from his pocket and searched through them. '"All these young people studying along-side me and making plans for the future want to achieve one thing: success and a name for themselves. A name amongst the nameless mass. They don't realise that in the depersonalised mass of the inferior there are no names, no individuality, no freedom."'

The judge put the letters back in his pocket. '"Depersonalised mass of the inferior." You have created a new concept, congratu-lations. The opposite of inferior is probably superior. The price for the superior being retaining his individuality must, it seems, be paid by others. Even with their life. Isn't that so?'

Janek said nothing.

'Believe it or not, your silence is eloquent.'

The priest once more drew near.

'Geder had problems,' he said. 'His wife left him. They had no children. He blamed her, she blamed him. She left and he began to chase everything in a skirt. He made fun of God. Twice I found him drunk in church. Give me a child, give me a child! Then he began to breed frogs. I don't know why frogs, exactly. At least this year he switched to chickens. Now…'

Suddenly embarrassed, the priest withdrew once more to his corner.

The investigating judge made a note in a small notebook that he drew from his other pocket, then he put it back. He turned again to Janek.

'With most murders, the killer and the victim know each other. Often, they are closely connected. Without any doubt, you were closely connected with Geder. Mutual creditors, mutual debtors. Mutual secrets, that you each carefully guarded. Every one of us is owed something and owes something to others, and sooner or later the creditor decides to collect his debt. And when that happens, it can all end very differently from how it was envisaged. Isn't that so?'

'Na janav ko dad mro has!' replied Janek. 'Niko malen mange has! Miro gule daj merdijas! Pirani man pregelijas!'

'I assume that's something in Romany. Or at least a language that's not on the school curriculum. So don't be offended if I don't know what you're trying to say. Or perhaps I do. Possibly, you're trying to tell me in a roundabout way that we must seek the causes of your peculiarities – and the troublesome presence of this corpse – in the fact that you have different blood in your veins and grew up in a different environment. Of course, someone will immediately accuse me of racism or chauvinism, so let's avoid that for now. Perhaps we can reach the agreement we seek along a different path. What do you say? Will you help me?'

Janek said nothing.

'Of course not. I'll have to do it on my own. It's a good job that I've already done half the work.' He once more pulled the papers from his pocket and went through them. 'I won't use the word Roma. I'll use the word gypsy, which is widely used in this area. Even the priest uses it. Here I have notes on the priest's opinion regarding the characteristics of the minority that you belong to. May I read it out?'

Janek said nothing.

'"The gypsy does not control his own nature, he constantly undermines himself and his principles. But he does this spontaneously, without evil intent. If he promises to come tomorrow to help with the harvest the promise is a serious one. But the next day it might happen that he doesn't come. If anyone accused him of lying they would be unjust, for when he swore he would come his intention was firm. But since the previous day much has changed. The sun has gone down, the moon has sailed across the sky, the sun has risen again, the wind has blown. And the gypsy thinks with the weather, he moves in the way that nature moves. His forebears' traditions reach back a thousand years, controlling him and his blood. His actions are dependent on coincidence, on the moment. There is nothing in the world that the gypsy clings to or completes."'

He folded the paper and returned it to his pocket.

'With one exception. Murder.'

Janek sat calmly on the floor and said not a word.

'Believe it or not,' continued the judge, 'I also visited one of your professors. I'm nothing if not thorough! It's in my blood. He told me a great deal about you, much more than I'd expected. "Professor, this university stinks, I don't want to be documented." That was what you said to him when you came to your exam and refused to answer any of his questions. He didn't drive you away, as I would have done if you'd tried anything that stupid with me. He was even friendly towards you. Do you remember his words? Of course not, how could you, if your head was already full of different ideas?'

Once more, he looked through the papers he drew from his pocket.

'"You're a very independent young man, a very rebellious young man, and I like that, I must admit… but a slightly more realistic view of the world would serve you better. You'll have to eat, you'll have a family… do you intend to leave university? What will you do, chop firewood, make bricks, sell newspapers? Climb over this barrier and when your future is guaranteed you can concern yourself with such thoughts as much as you like. Don't let your feelings lead you to make the wrong decision."'

He replaced the papers in his pocket.

'That's what your professor said. But you went your own way. The uncut umbilical cord drew you back. The call of your blood was stronger than your desire to flee from this archaic world, to grow up, to become one of us, to avoid the darkness and embrace the light. Why? Everyone was friendly towards you, everyone wanted to help you, in three years you'd be able to go around doing my job, asking the kind of questions that I must now ask you. We investigating judges are the advanced guard of a civilised society; we are entrusted with the task of cutting through the dark layer of concealment and silence beneath which flows a sick, parallel life, and to bring all that hides in the murky underground to the surface, the light, the sun. You were on the way, you had a goal.

What pulled you back? What would the world be like if we all dwelled in the darkness in which you sought refuge?'

'I don't know,' replied Janek. 'Better?'

'Your Ljubljana friend, who signs her letters, "always your Daria", reduced the concept of eternity to a more manageable timescale. In the interview I conducted with her she showed clearly that she regretted all the energy she invested in your relationship. But the relationship was an intense one, at least from her point of view, of that there's no doubt. From your side, perhaps a little less. In short, we're back where we should perhaps have stopped.'

Again he pulled out a letter from the pile: '"Your face is unusual, striking. I'm sure you must have been ugly when you were younger, for somewhere behind your current expression lie those features and they even sometimes leap to the foreground. Some kind of suffering gave you a disguise. That disguise is good-looking, people say, but there is hatred lurking beneath, violent hatred. That's the impression I get. Your face is more frightening than handsome. It fills me with horror. Because it is cruel. Maybe that's why women chase you. Have you thought of that? Do you feel hatred inside?"'

Janek got up and took a step towards the judge. 'That letter was addressed to me. Where did you get it?'

'So, you're speaking at last.'

'My personal things can be seized only with a warrant. Do you have one?'

'I'm an investigating judge, I can write one.'

'You can't. Even after only two years of study you learn what is in accordance with the law and what isn't. Besides which, I burned all my letters – where did you get something that no longer exists?'

'A great mystery, eh? Even greater than the murder we are investigating. But it will be easier for the two of us together, don't you think? We'll get to the bottom of things more quickly.'

'Some things don't have a bottom.'

'You mean things in the past?' The judge drew the papers from his pocket once more. '"If I knew your past very closely I could tell you why you are probably not responsible for some of your actions. You're ruled by your instincts, you live in the past, where your reason cannot reach. Your reason is limited and explicit. But the past you carry inside you is very strong. You are not aware that you react now as you reacted in the past… You were created by events. Nothing is as important for someone's state of mind as what he experienced in childhood.'"

'You've no idea…'

'That's true, so help me. I don't want to accuse you unfairly. It's a terrible thing when someone goes to prison for something he hasn't done.'

'She seemed beautiful to me. Daria in Ljubljana. Whenever I looked at her I felt satisfied. I always had the feeling that I had won some kind of victory. That something good had happened.'

'I understand…'

'She spoke to me in a simple way, without emphasis. As if we'd known each other for a long time. I got the feeling she was honest, that I could trust her. I needed that. I was alone. The city was very foreign.'

'A common feeling.'

'She visited me and spent whole afternoons. As soon as she came she stripped naked and walked about the room, lay in various poses, reading or talking with me. And the whole time I was forced to look at her nakedness. I was agitated, but after a week had passed, I got used to it. And then she said I had to get used to my own nakedness, and to her seeing me naked.'

'And?'

'Again, we spent whole afternoons sitting around in the room. Naked. And we watched each other. Then she said the time had come for… And so we… and stopped immediately.'

'Couldn't you do it?'

'I wanted to, desperately, but something… I crawled into a corner and started trembling. Out of fear, out of horror. I liked her, but… she wasn't the right one.'

'Not the right one?'

'No.'

'She wasn't it, the first one. The first and only one. The one in the past. From which you cannot escape. Who drags you back and pushes an axe into your hand so that you can chop down a centuries-old chestnut tree. And then a knife to stab the man who was in your way... Why was he in your way?'

'You wouldn't understand.'

The judge found another letter and read out: "'There's only one way. Your strange behaviour, your loathing arises from fear of sexuality. Why, I don't know. So I suggest we try. We make love. Perhaps with me you'll find that your fear, which you first experienced with your mother, is unjustified.'"

Janek slowly sank to his knees.

'Are we getting close?' asked the judge, leaning over him.

'On the evening of some morning or other, the wind once more smells of distant places,' recited Janek, staring into the distance. 'But I did not reach even the lower branches of the green chestnuts, and to this isolated house of God I have come to pray, although the altar is so empty, there are no saints, no angels, no virgin with a spotless halo, only a confessional; I kneel before it and wait at least for the small shadow from the wood to slide towards my grille, for me to admit: I have sinned, for I did not believe that the roots of the green chestnut trees are centuries-old; because I did not believe that the grass mates, loves and leaves like people, but never dies, only sleeps in the winter; and I did not believe that the sun can split into two smaller spheres, which sparkle in the emptiness and, somewhere out there, shine on. The shadow will never reach my grille, for all eternity I am confessing only to myself beneath the cupola of the chestnuts, and again on the evening of some morning or other, when the wind once more smells of distant places, only he has the sky in his eyes and the grass and the woods, only he perhaps knows that my green refuge is not a white figure with a scythe on its shoulder.'

The judge lit a cigarette.

'My dear Janek Hudorovec, since time is precious and since it is a sin for us to argue on this heavenly day, and since this case is crystal clear, I'd advise you to come to an understanding with me. What do you say?'

Janek said nothing, so the judge raised his voice.

'I arrived at nine and now it's two. I know everything about you, from the top of your head to your little toe. Let's come to an agreement: either you answer the questions or these two gentlemen will put you in the car and take you to prison. Whoever ends up there will have a hard time, as sure as I'm an investigating judge.'

'I've said all there is to say.'

'You told a story that even your own father wouldn't believe.'

'He certainly wouldn't.'

'I'll tell you what you did. First, you came here intending to slaughter him.'

'I made my plan ten years ago, when he pulled my ear.'

'Second, you quarrelled.'

'We pulled each other's hair and stuck our tongues out.'

'Third, during your quarrel you smashed everything in sight.'

'With an axe.'

'Fourth, you attacked him with a knife and plunged it into his heart!'

'I banged it into his chest with a hammer.'

'When he was dead, you pulled the knife out to fit with your little story! And then you crouched over the body all night, just to convince us – who you think are blind – that everything is just as it should be. Is that how it was?'

Janek said nothing; he was slumped on the floor, weak and flabby.

'Of course it was. But I want you to tell me yourself. To my face: Yes, I killed him.'

Janek said nothing.

'For the last time: answer, or I'll have to get rough!' He grabbed Janek by the shoulder. 'Come on lad!'

'Have you ever looked into the mirror?' Janek asked, staring into the judge's eyes.

The judge moved back in astonishment. 'Looked into – the what?'

'I did so last night. I wanted to see. Sadly, too late. For it happened that… I didn't see myself. I didn't see my face. I saw a large black stone. It glittered like, it glittered like...' He desperately sought a simile, but couldn't find one, so he called out in agony: 'Arrrgh! It glittered... glit... gli...' he began to choke, gasped and was then silent for a moment. 'There above it, in the sky, I saw two planets. Close together. And now I know. Most people live on one, I on the other.'

The judge stared at him for some moments, then he straightened up. 'It's clear that you are very confused.'

'My head is as clear as a crystal.'

'Crystals are not clear, they are cloudy.' He went over to the priest. 'Father, please repeat what you told me earlier.'

The priest hesitated. 'It doesn't seem... it doesn't seem exactly necessary.'

'I decide what is necessary and what is not. Did this young man turn vehemently against you and accuse you of peddling old wives' tales?'

'That is not important.'

'During questioning, you told me,' continued the judge, 'and it is written down, Father, that Hudorovec had undergone a change. He wounded you with his gross ingratitude. He slipped from your heart. If I am asking you to repeat that, why are you hesitating?'

The priest said nothing.

At this point, the judge moved over to a figure that had been hiding in the furthest corner:

'Aranka Hudorovec.'

'Sir Judge!' Aranka raised her tear-stricken face.

'Are you going to answer my questions?'

Aranka nodded.

'How long have you been having sexual relations with your son?'

'Oh, Sir Judge, I don't remember.'

'Ten years! You told me already, I have it written down.'

'Ten?'

'What about with the deceased, Geder? How long?'

Aranka's tears flowed freely. 'With Lojz? With Lojz, five years.'

'You hid your relationship with Geder from your son?'

'I did.'

'Why?'

'I was afraid he'd do something to him!'

'That your son might harm Geder?'

Aranka nodded.

'The day before yesterday you came here. You found them quarrelling. You son attacked Geder with a chair. Is that correct?'

Aranka nodded silently.

'And what did you do yesterday?'

'Yesterday?' Aranka raised her head.

'You told him you'd been sleeping with Geder!'

Aranka bowed her head. 'I did.'

'Why?'

'Because I'm with child!' she shrieked. She put her hands on her stomach and then pointed to Geder's corpse. 'With him! He's the father!'

Janek jumped up. 'She's lying! It's not true!'

With pleading eyes he turned to his mother. 'Mum?'

'It's true, son,' whimpered Aranka.

The investigating judge approached Janek. 'So now we know why you stabbed him.'

'With that... that... frog-breeder?'

Janek tried to throw himself at his mother, but the police officers restrained him. 'With that... dead slime? Nooo! Say it isn't true!'

Aranka shouted in despair: 'It's true, Janek, forgive me!'

With a sudden violent jerk Janek was free of the two police officers and standing in the middle of the room. He picked up the chestnut-leaf crown and put it on his head. He spun round. He raised his arms and shouted: 'Melalo! I'm ready! Let the golden toad come! Let him spray me with grey saliva! Let him close my eyes! Play and I will dance! I will dance three wild dances!'

He waited. Nothing happened.

There was complete silence in the room.

Janek bent over, then slid to the floor, groaning. Then he grabbed the crown and started to beat it like a madman, foaming at the mouth, making gargling noises. He only stopped when he was out of breath.

Aranka ran to him with a shriek and clung to him but Janek pushed her to the floor. 'Get away from me!' He went closer to the body and looked at it for some time. Then he looked at his mother, whose eyes were downcast. Finally, he sank on the floor next to Geder's corpse.

The judge slowly approached him. 'Well, Janek? Will you tell us?'

'I killed him,' replied Janek, quietly.

'You killed him,' said the judge after a short pause. 'Now please tell everyone here present what you did. Get up!'

Janek obeyed him mechanically. The judge turned him to face Aranka and then the priest. 'Say it.'

'I killed him,' said Janek again.

'Once more.'

'I killed him,' yelled Janek, as if out of his mind.

The judge gestured to the police officers. They took positions on either side of Janek, and led him out. He did not resist. He did not look at anyone, not even his mother. The judge reached for his hat, briefcase and jacket.

He gave a friendly smile. 'Everything's in order.'

He raised his hat and went out the door.

Light…

Why was that, actually? That he never saw anyone… Daria, for example? He saw her, but was unaware that he was seeing her. He did not sense it.

And now he remembered clearly.

Shades. Her walk.

That walk… He could find no words for it.

But he remembered clearly. An even, light, thoughtful walk… And her face. Her grey eyes. Sparse eyebrows. Eyelashes. Her forehead, which she would crease. Smooth hair that hung straight down. Cut. And her face was pale, always pale. Except when she blushed… That happened rarely.

She knew how to control herself.

If they walked together, she always took his hand. That was her habit. And her V-neck jumpers... Her bones protruded below her neck. Her breastbone. And breasts... she had large breasts. But otherwise, she was petite. And why did this woman now feel close to him?

He hears the priest's voice. His monotone, muffled voice.

And perhaps his features shine through the mist, his wide, rounded forehead, his sharp nose, his double chin, the paleness of his face. And his walk. He liked walking around the room when he spoke. With his hands behind his back. He stopped here or there, and then walked again.

Convincing himself that he could move. And yet now somewhere everything was final... And complete... No more need for excuses.

Or self-deceit.

The moment when the rules of the game demand consequences.

A victim.

A sense.

Because that must be the point of the game. That it handcuffs you the moment you want to escape.

And then...

When the need for excuses vanishes... Is it then still necessary to think? Is it necessary to wade through the murky rivers of memory? It becomes nauseating. A person grows weary. The rock shackles him. He cannot lift his arm.

And the greatest nausea is caused by clean things...

Snow.

Damp. Crystalline. Soft. Fluffy. The wind...

Nothing evokes fear anymore. Nothing evokes memory. Everything is exhausting. Everything is a burden.

Everything awakens nausea.

Is this what is left of a person at the end of the game?

Everything ground up? A rag?

A rag turned to stone. For the wind collides with it and cannot move it.

The wind whistles around corners.

The wind dusts the wide, empty streets with snow. And on towards the north.

There prevails in life a basic tone that leaks through all the added layers. A basic colour. Live particles of dust. That may be the right… that may be it…

Obscure.

It's impossible to find the words…

It's a smell. A smell of the sun, grass, the closeness of evening, the wind. And the water moving lazily in the stream. And the waves of spruce forests… The shrieks of dirty children from the valley… The smoke from a settlement… A dog barks…

That's the smell… The gypsy smell.

Mother's.

That's all that is left.

Mother's.

Everything else has gone.

No feelings. No thoughts. No restlessness.

No goal.

And so no restlessness…

A person is restless only when he thinks about the future… Of possible outcomes… Of a changed past he presents to himself.

Then comes the dead point. Immobility.

Death.

Then that long path…

First a wide road. Hollow and white. Far. At its end, through the falling veil of snow, shine the pale street lights. Struggling along the old trails are solitary black birds. Bent over, worn out.

Not one of them stops, not one opens its beak.

Macabre. Exhausted.

Evening birds.

Then the plain.

Endless.

And white.

The wind raises white dust, carries it through the air, deposits it elsewhere, creates drifts. Then spits it in your face, whistling.

Gusting.

Sombre.

Dying down in the unseen expanse.

And arising again. The path is long. It lasts long into the night. Legs numb. Then when there is nothing left inside, only nature, but not even that, only its shadow… far, from a great distance… Then all words are extremely old, unimportant…

There are no new names. Only floating pictures, a floating expanse.

Floating indifference.

Somewhere, deep down, drowned long ago… Fury… Seeking… And will…

And horror.

And flight.

Return home. There, where it all happened. Began and ended.

Escaping from jail is not difficult.

Escaping your fate? Impossible.

The stars are finally shining. And the sky is bluish. Where does that bluish tinge come from… And the pines rustle… There's a slight wind. And far off, the plain. And it is white like a painted surface…

Cold splashes from the sky.

Sharp…

And here's a settlement.

Here are houses. Here's a wooded slope. Here a valley. And a stream.

And silence.

This is that world.

There the Baranjas sleep. There the Horvats. There the Šarkezis. Packed together.

They warm each other with their bodies. Brothers and sisters play secret night games. And it's warm.

But outside it's cold. And mother…

In that house sleeps mother.

And higher up, Geder's empty house. And even further… The church…. The presbytery.

The priest by the stove, reading a book. He walks about the room…

 Peace…

No dog…

That's it. The past. Absence. Death.

That you no longer have. That you no longer have anything to think about.

That you have no future. And cannot seek for more.

A worthless word. Seek…

Twenty years there? Or twenty years here?

It's now just a question of effort! To cause twenty years of effort.

In this world, certainly! Outside…

Outside, you must keep seeking freedom. Space. And those are fruitless urges.

A pointless exercise.

A vicious circle.

And here you must keep trying again to see yourself. To make sense.

To be.

And you do not reach the end.

But there, behind the walls, it is determined!

There, the whole pointlessness is clear. So you try nothing and do not really live. And it is less demanding there. It is pleasant in the end to lie down inside the great jaws and fall asleep…

Safe… and warm.

And forsake yourself, drain your blood.

Because outside… outside it is cold…

And outside, what you wish for isn't there.

Twenty years of death is more certain than a year of life.

 And so back… Back to prison.

When summer came, the desire for free movement reappeared. It became ever stronger. Escaping once more was no more difficult than the first time.

But this time, he did not go home, he went to the seaside. Even sinners deserve a summer holiday. Each day he went along the rocky path into the hills, where he sat and looked at the bay beneath him. A feeling began to sneak into him that he was unfamiliar with: something comfortable, pleasant, a kind of satisfaction. He could clearly feel the dullness inside him crumbling away, and a strange restlessness was flowing into him, causing him to become agitated by the waves below him. The waves seemed to flow from the distant mountains, across the bay, towards the coast and stopped at the white cliffs. At moments it seemed as if the island to his right was also covered with lines of waves, that the island was also moving somewhere. He felt the wind blow around him, catching in his hair; he tried to see the waves in the air, for it seemed as if the wind was moving through the air in the same way. Then the wind retreated, the island became calm, reflecting the blinding white sun from white rocks. Then the sea became smooth, for there was always a calm period around midday, and the sun began to burn. When his head had almost sunk to his chest from tiredness, he gathered up his last ounce of strength, got to his feet and staggered down the hill.

And he returned to his room.

He stood at the open window. Outside lay the sea in the hot afternoon sun. From the beach could be heard the shouts of children and the gentle splash of the waves, which had begun to beat against the rocks below the hostel. On the terrace below him, a waiter moving tables, shaking tablecloths and smoothing them out. Then another appeared with a sweeping brush. The mountains on the other side of the bay disappeared in the afternoon haze. It seemed as if the sea arose from the thin horizon and was slowly travelling towards the shore. A boat slipped by below him. Two women with big straw hats were sitting at the shoreline, their feet in the water. The bald patch of the man rowing shone in the sun. The leafy trees in front of the hostel threw large shadows on the terrace and the immediate surroundings seemed cold, separated from the world outside with its bright sunshine and the shouts of children in the sea. Here, everything was torpid, even the waiters below moved stiffly, their faces blank, moving here and there like robots. From somewhere, he wasn't sure exactly where, behind the hostel or down on the road, came the weary sound of cicadas, but they immediately fell silent again. Yet perhaps they had not fallen silent, perhaps his attention had focused on something else and he no longer heard them.

He did not know how long he stood like that. The world flowed into him, wave after wave splashed across his eyes, he was breathing in all this material matter that floated in his retina, he felt how the sea flooded his lungs and then receded, steadily, in lines of waves; on the back of his neck he felt something cold – probably the wind, because the treetops were restless. Then he left the window, went out through the door, down the stairs and across the terrace, past the two waiters. He stepped over a heap of dust that they had swept to the edge, went down the steps and onto the dusty road. Dust rose beneath his steps and rose around him, quite high, almost forcing its way into his eyes and mouth. He came to the first street and turned left. Here there was no longer any dust. On the tightly-laid paving stones he headed towards the church on the hill.

The higher he went, the clearer were the cries of the children on the beach. Then the noise faded, became ever more distant. The sound of the sea, somewhere far below his feet, kept splashing against his ears, and the cicadas sprang into song right next to the path and then fell silent again. The silence went with him until his footsteps disturbed it. Then, in the distance, once more came children's voices from the beach. He was nearing the church, the path zigzagging its way up. One moment the sea was behind him, the next he could see it below him, each time further away. The red roofs of the houses clustered together and the people on the pier crawled like black ants. Just before the church he stopped and looked towards the island on the right. It seemed more sandy than usual. Grey layers of some kind of dust covered its slopes. Now that he was high up, he saw that the sea behind the island stretched to the misty horizon. Here and there on the water floated white foam. The boats in the bay were moving at snail's pace, their engines almost inaudible, quietly humming. He went on, turning left at the church, leaving behind him the stone-walled graveyard and heading towards the blueberry bushes growing on the hilltop. As he got closer, he breathed deeply. The climb had taken it out of him, but he wasn't clearly aware of this. He came to the point where the path slowly began to drop down, for the hill now sloped gently towards the other side. Here he stopped and looked around.

First there swam from his eyes the tall grass whose seed heads hung in the air before him, then the bushes that grew slightly further away disappeared, then the band of sea behind the hill tore and the air was extinguished, the world floated away from his senses and he could no longer hear. First there was a drumming in his ears as if the air was rent asunder, then silence like the grave. When it moved away, he felt as if his being was growing again, that his substance was filling all the space around him. It was as if he was becoming naked substance that felt only itself. He resisted this submergence… he wanted to cling to the wall, but he slipped back; he saw Daria holding out her hand, knew that she wanted to help him, he took hold of the hand, squeezed it, and then, when he was at the top of the wall, he was carried to the other side, and he grabbed Daria by the throat so as not to fall, he held on.

Gradually he calmed down, he returned from his body, the world began to flow into him once more, he saw the bushes in front of him, he saw the band of grey sea.

Further on should have been the sky.

But he saw nothing.

He rose and went slowly, as he had come, among the sparse bushes back to the path, then to the place where the hill peaked. He began to go back down towards the church. Once again, the bay lay beneath him. He saw the long white beach, where the choppy afternoon waves were breaking; he saw the ant-like people moving lazily on the pier. The boats were still gliding noiselessly across the water. On the island to the right lay the shadow of some kind of dust. He went back towards the sea. The church was behind him, his ears were once more assailed by children's shouts. He took a few more long steps.

Then he crumpled.

He lay on the sharp rocks. Through his mind swam the excruciating thought that he should get up and carry on, to the water, but it flapped its fragile wings ever more weakly and was lost. He saw the long beach full of bathers. It suddenly seemed to him as if it was packed with people, crawling all over each other. They transformed into dust and the dust was swarming; he looked at the pier and there, too, he saw a swarm of dust. The sea changed into blackish dust that swarmed like billions of tiny creatures. It was flowing towards the shore in straight lines. It flooded the town and crept up the hill. He still had a clear awareness, he was still trying to rise and flee back up the hill, for the flood of dust was coming closer. It reached his face, his lips. The specks of dust swarmed across him. They were neither warm nor cold.

He felt that he would again have to return to the safety of prison.

And remain there.

THE AUTHOR

Evald Flisar is a novelist, playwright, essayist, editor and globe-trotter. He worked as an underground train driver in Sydney, an editor of an encyclopaedia of science and invention in London, an author of short stories and radio plays for the BBC, and was president of the Slovene Writers' Association (1995–2002). Since 1998 he has been the chief editor of the oldest Slovenian literary journal Sodobnost (Contemporary Review). He is the author of fifteen novels (ten of them short-listed for the 'Kresnik' prize, the Slovenian 'Booker'), two collections of short stories, three travelogues, two books for children, and fifteen stage plays (eight nominated for Best Play of the Year Award, three winners). He is also the recipient of the Prešeren Foundation Prize, the highest state award for prose and drama and the prestigious Župančič Award for lifetime achievement. His various works have been translated into forty-one languages, among them Bengali, Malay, Nepalese, Indonesian, Turkish, Greek, Japanese, Chinese, Arabic, Czech, Albanian, Lithuanian, Icelandic, Romanian, Amharic, Russian, English, German, Italian and Spanish. His stage plays are regularly performed all over the world, most recently in Austria, Russia, USA, India, Indonesia, Japan, Taiwan, Serbia, Bosnia and Belarus. Throughout his career he has attended more than fifty literary readings and festivals on all continents. After a long period of life abroad (three years in Australia, seventeen years in London), Flisar has been resident in Ljubljana, Slovenia, since 1990. In 2014, his novel 'On the Gold Coast' (published in English by Sampark, Kolkata, India) was nominated for one of the most prestigious European literary prizes, the Dublin International Literary Award. Eileen Battersby of The Irish Times included it in her list of thirteen best novels about Africa written by Europeans; alongside Joseph Conrad and Graham Greene.

THE TRANSLATOR

David Limon translates literature for children and adults from Slovene into English. His translations include five novels by the internationally recognised author Evald Flisar. He has also translated short stories or other works by a range of writers including Fran Levstik, Ivan Cankar, Janez Trdina, Vitomil Zupan, Mirana Likar Bajželj, Tadej Golob, Lenart Zajc, Jani Virk, Nina Kokelj, Jana Bauer, Janja Vidmar and Desa Muck. He is Associate Professor at the Department of Translation at the University of Ljubljana.